PRAISE FOR

Tom Clancy fans open to a strong female lead will clamor for more.

— *Drone*, Publishers Weekly

Superb! Miranda is utterly compelling!

— *Booklist,* starred review

Miranda Chase continues to astound and charm.

— Barb M.

Escape Rating: A. Five Stars! OMG just start with *Drone* and be prepared for a fantastic binge-read!

— Reading Reality

The best military thriller I've read in a very long time. Love the female characters.

— *Drone,* Sheldon McArthur, founder of The Mystery Bookstore, LA

A fabulous soaring thriller.

— *TAKE OVER AT MIDNIGHT,* MIDWEST BOOK
REVIEW

Meticulously researched, hard-hitting, and suspenseful.

— *PURE HEAT,* PUBLISHERS WEEKLY, STARRED
REVIEW

Expert technical details abound, as do realistic military missions with superb imagery that will have readers feeling as if they are right there in the midst and on the edges of their seats.

— *LIGHT UP THE NIGHT,* RT REVIEWS, 4 1/2 STARS

Buchman has catapulted his way to the top tier of my favorite authors.

— FRESH FICTION

Nonstop action that will keep readers on the edge of their seats.

— *TAKE OVER AT MIDNIGHT,* LIBRARY JOURNAL

M L. Buchman's ability to keep the reader right in the middle of the action is amazing.

— Long and Short Reviews

The only thing you'll ask yourself is, "When does the next one come out?"

— *Wait Until Midnight,* RT Reviews, 4 stars

The first...of (a) stellar, long-running (military) romantic suspense series.

— *The Night is Mine,* Booklist, "The 20 Best Romantic Suspense Novels: Modern Masterpieces"

I knew the books would be good, but I didn't realize how good.

— Night Stalkers series, Kirkus Reviews

Buchman mixes adrenalin-spiking battles and brusque military jargon with a sensitive approach.

— Publishers Weekly

13 times "Top Pick of the Month"

— Night Owl Reviews

START THE CHASE

A MIRANDA CHASE POLITICAL
TECHNOTHRILLER ANTHOLOGY

M. L. BUCHMAN

SIGN UP FOR M. L. BUCHMAN'S NEWSLETTER TODAY

and receive:
Release News
Free Short Stories
a Free Book

Get your free book today. Do it now.
free-book.mlbuchman.com

CONTENTS

Also by M. L. Buchman   xi
About This Book   xiii

MIRANDA'S HIGH PASSAGE   1
HOLLY GAMES A NEW PATH   37
MIKE'S LAST BIG CON   79
JEREMY FINDS HIS FEET   135
ANDI DISCOVERS WHAT'S IN A NAME   173
TAZ FLIES HER COLORS   223
Afterword   277
The Process   279
Miranda Chase so far   281
MIRANDA CHASE #10 (EXCERPT)   283

About the Author   297
Also by M. L. Buchman   299
Sign up for M. L. Buchman's newsletter today   301
Play The Game   303

Other works by M. L. Buchman: (* - also in audio)

Action-Adventure Thrillers

Dead Chef
One Chef!
Two Chef!

Miranda Chase
Drone*
Thunderbolt*
Condor*
Ghostrider*
Raider*
Chinook*
Havoc*
White Top*

Romantic Suspense

Delta Force
Target Engaged*
Heart Strike*
Wild Justice*
Midnight Trust*

Firehawks
MAIN FLIGHT
Pure Heat
Full Blaze
Hot Point*
Flash of Fire*
Wild Fire
SMOKEJUMPERS
Wildfire at Dawn*
Wildfire at Larch Creek*
Wildfire on the Skagit*

The Night Stalkers
MAIN FLIGHT
The Night Is Mine
I Own the Dawn
Wait Until Dark
Take Over at Midnight

Light Up the Night
Bring On the Dusk
By Break of Day
AND THE NAVY
Christmas at Steel Beach
Christmas at Peleliu Cove
WHITE HOUSE HOLIDAY
Daniel's Christmas*
Frank's Independence Day*
Peter's Christmas*
Zachary's Christmas*
Roy's Independence Day*
Damien's Christmas*
5E
Target of the Heart
Target Lock on Love
Target of Mine
Target of One's Own

Shadow Force: Psi
At the Slightest Sound*
At the Quietest Word*
At the Merest Glance*
At the Clearest Sensation*

White House Protection Force
Off the Leash*
On Your Mark*
In the Weeds*

Contemporary Romance

Eagle Cove
Return to Eagle Cove
Recipe for Eagle Cove
Longing for Eagle Cove
Keepsake for Eagle Cove

Henderson's Ranch
Nathan's Big Sky*
Big Sky, Loyal Heart*
Big Sky Dog Whisperer*

Other works by M. L. Buchman:

Contemporary Romance (cont)

Love Abroad
Heart of the Cotswolds: England
Path of Love: Cinque Terre, Italy

Where Dreams
Where Dreams are Born
Where Dreams Reside
Where Dreams Are of Christmas*
Where Dreams Unfold
Where Dreams Are Written

Science Fiction / Fantasy

Deities Anonymous
Cookbook from Hell: Reheated
Saviors 101

Single Titles
The Nara Reaction
Monk's Maze
the Me and Elsie Chronicles

Non-Fiction

Strategies for Success
Managing Your Inner Artist/Writer
Estate Planning for Authors*
Character Voice
Narrate and Record Your Own Audiobook*

Short Story Series by M. L. Buchman:

Romantic Suspense

Delta Force
Th Delta Force Shooters
The Delta Force Warriors

Firehawks
The Firehawks Lookouts
The Firehawks Hotshots
The Firebirds

The Night Stalkers
The Night Stalkers 5D Stories
The Night Stalkers 5E Stories
The Night Stalkers CSAR
The Night Stalkers Wedding Stories

US Coast Guard

White House Protection Force

Contemporary Romance

Eagle Cove

Henderson's Ranch*

Where Dreams

Action-Adventure Thrillers

Dead Chef

Miranda Chase Origin Stories

Science Fiction / Fantasy

Deities Anonymous

Other
The Future Night Stalkers
Single Titles

ABOUT THIS BOOK

Before they were the hottest, and most at-risk, air-crash investigation team for the NTSB and the US military, the six members of Miranda Chase's team had each started along very unique paths.

Courtesy of backers of The Great Chase *tabletop game Kickstarter, their pasts are revealed. Discover why each team member's future turned out so differently than they planned.*

Six riveting stories filled with challenges, disasters, and triumphs.

They are in order by when each character joins Miranda's team in the series. All except the first story guest stars the patrons who pledged their support. Miranda, as so often happens, stands alone.

MIRANDA'S HIGH PASSAGE

Long before Miranda Chase became a top military-crash investigator for the NTSB, she learned to fly.

When the engine of her dead father's beloved airplane fails over the remote Idaho wilderness, it takes every ounce of her piloting skills to survive the landing. With the potential for rescue an unknown variable, her habits as a high-functioning autistic take over. She aims all of her focus to solving the cause of her own crash.

Her survival? That's another matter entirely.

1

September 19th, 2003
Bitterroot Wilderness, Idaho
Elevation: 6,853 feet

SHE WAS ALIVE!

Miranda Chase decided that constituted a surprising assessment—and a wholly unexpected one given the circumstances.

She kept her hands on the control yoke as the last shudder of the crash rippled through the plane's airframe. Outside the cockpit windows, a tall Douglas fir considered its options. Thrive or—

Not!

Unable to survive the impact of stopping her Mooney 201 four-seat aircraft, sixty feet of eight-inch diameter fir tree broke at the point of impact of her propeller's center spinner. At thirty-one pounds per cubic foot, it weighed more than half as much as her plane. Thankfully, it fell twenty degrees to the left, rather than testing the crushability of her plane's already battered fuselage—and herself.

She followed its fall as well as she could through the snow it had spattered over the windscreen when she'd hit it at the end of her long skid across the snowfield.

When the tree impacted the port wing, her plane shuddered with a final death throe. Three separate branches punched through the thin aluminum sheet metal as if determined to pin her to the ground beyond anything the crash had achieved. All three punctures lay outboard of the mid-wing seam, so it was unlikely any of them would have punctured the long-range fuel tanks. The inboard ones would be completely safe.

Out the windscreen, the gap left by the fallen tree revealed only more snow-shrouded pines. The early-morning sun hadn't yet cleared the peaks, but the sky was bright blue above the towering walls of fir-green and snow-white.

She reached over to shut down the avionics—she'd already pulled the throttle and set the fuel valve to Off moments before the crash as a precaution against fire per Section 3 Page 8 of the Pilot's Operating Handbook, "Gear-Up Landing"—but she couldn't seem to free her hands from the yoke.

Staring at them didn't help. Her fingers remained clenched white, a sharp contrast to the black plastic of the uprights. In fact, they were beginning to hurt they were clenched so hard.

Still no give.

When her breath exploded out of her, she realized that

she'd been holding it since the moment before the belly of her Mooney 201 had impacted the snow.

She dragged in a deep breath.

It was rich with the scent of pine, and already it tasted cooler than it had aloft.

She closed the air vent to conserve heat, then looked at her hands in surprise.

"*Now* you can move?"

Before they changed their mind to once more being out of her control, she began shutting down the plane's systems.

The transponder was set to 7700, exactly as it should be for an emergency.

But she'd delayed. Perhaps too long.

At the first cough of the engine, she'd begun her troubleshooting in the traditional reverse-question mark path that her father had taught her long before she was tall enough for her feet to reach the rudder pedals. To remind herself of that, she always wrote her question marks from the dot upward.

The period on the floor was the fuel tank selector. Switching it between tanks hadn't helped because she had plenty of av-gas in both tanks. Straight above, auxiliary fuel pump—no improvement. Curve to check mixture control and throttle. The final arc, past where the shaft of the yoke penetrated the main panel, to the left-hand magneto switch —from Both to Right to Both to Left, then back to Both when there was no change.

Nothing had worked.

So she'd done the second question mark: pull the fuel dump "gascolator" by her feet for five seconds to purge any accumulated water or sediment, then check the cowl flap, the alternate air, and finally the instruments for any additional clues.

There hadn't been any except for the rapidly falling engine rpm.

A second cycle through the two question marks of recovery hadn't improved the results. Dad had always taught her to check everything important twice, but that the third time was a waste of effort. Even at twenty it was hard for her to resist the urge to repeat actions a third time, but she'd learned.

The engine had stuttered one last time and, with a muffled bang, died high above the color blocking of dark green and blinding white of the Idaho wilderness.

The silence had seemed far louder than the familiar thrum of the Lycoming IO-360 four-cylinder engine.

The propeller had hung, motionless and mute, against a broad vista of snowy peaks and thick forest. She was truly in the heart of the wilderness.

The Air Start Procedure hadn't achieved the slightest cough from the engine, just the high whine of the struggling starter motor.

She'd finally done the third question mark that was not a repeat of the first two: fuel valve off, throttle pulled out, transponder to the emergency frequency of 7700, then shut down of the electrical system.

Which had shut down the power to the transponder.

Should she have called "Mayday" before she'd done that?

Nothing in the manual addressed that.

She didn't like talking to people anyway. Based on her study of her past interactions with people, over sixty-seven percent of those interactions had added more confusion than they resolved. The number jumped to eighty-three if she factored out her dead parents and Tante Daniels who'd been her guardian until her eighteenth birthday two years ago.

Now that she'd crashed, she admitted that her desire to not engage had perhaps been ill-considered. Her autism spectrum disorder made her seek the familiar but, in this instance, had it over-shielded her from possible aid?

Did that constitute pilot error in the crash?

No. The plane had already failed and was going down. At least that aspect of pilot error could be crossed off the list of possible causes.

Besides she'd had very little time.

From maximum cruise altitude without oxygen at twelve thousand five hundred feet, until she'd dropped below the top of Trapper Peak at over ten thousand had taken less than three minutes, even holding best rate-of-glide. Three more had seen her on the ground in a dead plane somewhere in the Idaho wilderness. Now pinned to the snow by a fallen tree. Outside it was past sunrise, but she could see by the shadows that she'd soon be losing the sun from her narrow, east-facing valley.

The more she considered it, the more convinced she became that she should have called someone.

Flipping to a fresh page of her personal notebook, she made an entry to remember to ask for assistance in emergency situations. Her pen poised over "emergency." Would "complex" be a better adjective?

Unsure, she let the entry stand as it was written.

2

SHE REPOWERED THE RADIO. IT APPEARED TO WORK, BUT NO one was responding out here in the middle of the wilderness. Her mobile phone had no signal indicators. While national cellular coverage had improved greatly in the first three years of the new millennium, as far as she knew there was still no coverage between Washington State and Iowa. And she was in central Idaho.

From her current position along a valley floor, no airport was going to detect her emergency signal. And the transponder only responded when it was probed by a ground radar.

She switched it off to save the battery.

In case the crash hadn't been sufficiently violent—five to seven g's were required to trigger the ELT—she turned the Emergency Locator Transmitter from ARM to ON. Up above, the sky was a blank blue. She hadn't crashed along a major air route. It would be chance at best if an airliner spotted her signal. That meant it was up to a satellite pass, that was listening on the correct frequency, to pick up a weak signal from the ground. It was the best she could do with the existing systems.

What next? What next?

Wracking her brain didn't help.

Her hands had drifted back to the yoke to hold on; their grip slowly tightened once more until she could feel her throbbing pulse in every finger.

Perfect. Just perfect. She felt as if she'd been holding on too tightly for years.

Ever since her parents' death on flight TWA 800 when she was thirteen, she'd studied NTSB reports. But when the National Transportation Safety Board ran an investigation, it generally stopped tracking events at the same time the plane stopped moving, unless there was a fire.

Miranda looked out both windows and sniffed the air.

No sign of fire.

She had no guidance from them of what to do next.

Is that what they'd teach her at the NTSB Academy? The first class started in just three days and she didn't want to be late. She'd left an extra day for the cross-country flight to ensure that she wouldn't be.

She looked at the clock. She should be over Missoula, Montana by now. They had an airport. She could have landed there if her plane had failed now.

But it hadn't.

It had failed here.

At what time? She hadn't noted the time.

She wouldn't be able to note the exact time of the crash. Or properly note her flight time in her logbook. Had she been on the ground for five minutes, or fifteen?

It was easy enough to calculate the time from the engine failure to the landing—six minutes. Would it be acceptable to declare the time of engine failure by calculation rather than observation?

To be sure, she pulled out the Seattle and the Great Falls Sectional Aeronautical Charts, her ruler, and a notepad. She had her departure time from the airport on her family's island in the San Juans of Puget Sound, Washington written in her log book.

Four minutes from engine start to takeoff. No, seven. She'd had to wait for a doe and her young fawn to clear the runway before she departed.

She calculated climb rates at present fuel loads and distance traveled. At economy cruise she would have had a transit time of two hours and eight minutes to her position near Trapper Peak. The descent, she back-calculated the six minutes of the gliding descent.

Miranda studied the dashboard clock, then double-checked it against her watch.

Was it a reasonable assumption that she'd crashed twenty-three minutes ago?

She didn't think so. Her best estimate was less than five minutes had elapsed.

Then she noticed that she could see her breath in the cabin and had to suppress a shiver. It was unlikely for the plane to cool so much in just five minutes, or even twenty-three.

And how long had it taken her to do the calculations. Time always slipped by so easily when she was working on math or cryptography.

So, she noted down the calculated time, and then added

a footnote of the eighteen-minute differential, then attached her calculations to the logbook in case an FAA inspector ever had any questions about the accuracy of her accumulated flight hours.

She made a second copy for the Accident Report file. If only she'd thought to bring a manila folder so that she could start one properly. But, beyond general preparedness for a cross-country flight, she hadn't thought ahead about the possibility of a crash. It wasn't a mistake she'd make again.

Once she'd completed that and restowed everything properly, she reached into the back seat and retrieved her jacket.

3

WHEN HER HANDS ATTEMPTED TO DRIFT BACK TO THE STEERING yoke, she forced them onto her lap.

She had planned for this transition to joining the NTSB so carefully, each step laid out and reviewed until it was as clear as an air route in her head. She'd even drawn it up as if it was a flight plan for her life.

Miranda had completed both of her masters degrees in June. She'd spent the next ten weeks working on her Aircraft Maintenance Engineer course. Two weeks had been allowed on Spieden Island, as the family home was the only place she could be truly alone. For two weeks she done everything she could to prepare herself for this next phase.

Joining the NTSB was going to be her first job and it was the one thing she needed to do perfectly. Perfectly, or more people might die like her parents.

She had never in her life *not* been studying.

Her very first memory was of herself and her father in the family garden. He'd been installing a bronze sculpture covered in letters. It was like a wavy piece of paper, on edge, but thick and as tall as she was.

"You'll learn to read this, Miranda. It's a secret code and we'll work on it together until it's done."

He'd been wrong, but not unfairly. Death had taken him before they'd broken any of the codes hidden in the sculpture.

Now she was going to her final school, the brand-new NTSB Academy.

Would they teach her what to do after a crash was done crashing?

Yes.

Yes, they would.

Granted, she had arrived on this scene as the actual pilot of the plane crash. Had other NTSB investigators arrived at the site of a crash this way? A quick mental review didn't bring any to mind.

Retrieving her Toshiba Satellite laptop from her flight bag, she booted to the index she'd made of every NTSB report. She hadn't cross-indexed them based on the inspector first being the pilot of the crash, but she tried several searches of her notes with no results.

Of course, she wasn't technically an NTSB inspector yet.

However, she knew what came next.

The crash investigation.

That would require warmer clothes.

She slipped out of her left-hand seat and into the copilot's right-hand one to open the door.

Outside, the air was a cold slap as she stepped out onto the grip strip on the wing. A light breeze drifted needles of snow against her cheeks. She shut the cabin door behind her to keep the snow out.

Her breathing was still fast, but she had no way to judge if that was due to the crash or the unexpected altitude. The highest point on her island was under four hundred feet above sea level. She had been flying in an unpressurized cabin at twelve-five for nearly two hours, so perhaps it was the crash.

Or perhaps it was the quality of the air, not its thinness.

It was so different here. Off the Pacific, the wind blew fresh as if it had just been created for her alone, scrubbed by its five-thousand-mile journey over seawater. Here there was a sharp Arctic clarity to it that made her want to breathe deeply and fill her lungs with its edgy chill.

She turned to her father to tell him about it, but he wasn't here. He'd been dead for seven years but she couldn't break the habit.

Dad was the one she'd always turned to when she'd learned something new. Perhaps because he had always pushed her to learn new things. Mom had taught her how to *do* things: dress, eat, ignore bullies (or at least survive them).

Mom was all about the day-to-day parts of life.

Dad was the imagination. Sam Chase had been a...a... fountain of imagination. Metaphors had always been a challenge for her and Miranda was particularly pleased with that one.

Olivia Holmes Chase had been... But she couldn't find a good comparison for Mom.

Miranda had barely heard of the NTSB when they'd died in the explosion and crash.

But since that day, it had become her life's blood. The

sole focus that allowed her to handle everything else that was happening around her. With Tante Daniels' help she'd gotten through life. With her father's imagination still driving her, she'd graduated high school three years early, earned her dual masters in Materials Science and Aeronautical Engineering, and successfully found a job at the NTSB.

A job that was supposed to start in three days with classes at the Academy.

Now was the time of transition. She was twenty and would be twenty-one by the time she completed her studies at the Academy. It was time to stop learning and start doing.

She checked her watch. Billings, Montana was supposed to be passing beneath her wings in the next four minutes.

Except that was the original Flight Plan. Now it had to be revised.

After Billings, it would be another thirty-seven minutes to...

Recognizing the loop that her mind was entering, she used one of the tools Mom had taught her.

"WWDD?"

A Steller's Jay fluttered down to perch on the plane's upright rudder. Its dark blue body and black head stood out starkly against the snowy backdrop and the white rudder top. She had some trail mix, but she'd left it inside the plane. If it was like the Steller's Jays on her island, any effort to fetch the food would spook it away.

"What would Dad do?" she asked it instead of feeding it.

It considered Miranda's question, rubbed its beak on either side of the rudder, then offered its loud call of, "What! What! What! What! What!" Birding guides insisted that the call was "Chook" but it had always sounded like "What" to her. Her father had agreed, saying that was a correct call.

"That's my question," she told the jay since her father wasn't here to make suggestions.

It repeated the call, then was gone in a quick flutter of dark wings.

Sam Chase had always pushed her to understand why things worked the way they did.

Cryptographic codes had been only one aspect his codebreaking lessons. Math, probability, even card games had been added on to that.

When he'd taught her to hunt, it had included weeks of study: everything from gun safety to ballistics and loading her own rounds.

Flying wasn't only about the navigator and pilot roles, but also the mechanic's. That had extended into the new satellite-fed GPS system. For her tenth birthday, he'd given her a receiver and used that as a springboard for lessons in space launch and orbital mechanics.

What *would* her father do?

He'd want to know the same thing the NTSB would want to know: what had gone wrong with his airplane that had caused it to crash in the Idaho wilderness?

Now that her path was clear, she opened the baggage hatch and pulled out heavier clothes. Uncertain of Washington, DC's winters, she'd packed her heavy winter gear from when Dad had taken her winter hiking on Hurricane Ridge on Washington's Olympic Peninsula.

Like most of her clothes, she hadn't outgrown them. She'd reached five-two by the age of twelve. The two inches she'd grown since hadn't affected the size of her parka.

A quick check, obviously there was no one to watch her change.

Absolutely no one for twenty or thirty miles.

The girls' locker room for gym class had always been one of her horrors. It was one of the main reasons she'd worked so hard to finish high school three years early— that and her need to start making sure plane accidents didn't kill any of her friends' parents. If she'd had any friends.

Sitting on the wing, she also donned snow pants and boots.

Then she pulled out her prized new possession. How many hours had she spent considering the accumulated clues contained within the various NTSB reports?

It would be the first time she'd worn it other than in front of the mirror.

Taking a deep breath, she pulled it on.

The custom vest was tight, especially over her parka, but that was okay, she liked the pressure, the sureness of its embrace.

She checked the pockets one by one: notebooks, two micro-recorders, anemometer, voltmeter, a variety of pliers and other small tools, even plastic evidence bags and numbered markers for photographs.

Finally she looped the leather badge holder over her neck. She didn't have an official ID to store in it yet. That worried her. She *had* called ahead to ascertain the proper dimensions before purchasing the holder, but the ID itself wouldn't be issued until she arrived at the new job.

She reached over her back to rub the six-inch reflective-yellow letters there: NTSB.

Was it wrong to wear the vest before she actually started her employment?

But she couldn't figure out how to proceed with the investigation without the vest.

Hoping that it didn't get her into trouble with anyone, she left it on.

Yes. Miranda Chase was definitely a different person *in* the vest than out of it. For the first time since her parents' death, she once again belonged to something bigger than herself.

Motivating herself had always been a challenge. There were whole years where her life would have been far easier and all of them would have been more comfortable if she never left her bedroom. But not living up to her father's standards wasn't an option. He and Mom had both always made her successes so important that she'd never wanted to disappoint them.

Tante Daniels had taken some of that role, that and not wanting to disappoint her parents even if they were dead. Now there would once again be a group where excelling was something more than getting good grades. It would be making aviation safer for everyone—one crash at a time.

And it was time to focus on this crash.

She carefully folded her lightweight flying jacket and stowed it with her luggage.

Closing the hatch, she stood once more on the wing.

The Steller's Jay hadn't returned, but she'd answered his question anyway. Miranda knew what to do now.

She was a crash investigator and her plane had crashed. It was time to investigate it. For her initial inspection she would follow the same route as a preflight inspection.

Step One per Section Four Page Two of the Pilot's Operating Handbook specified that a preflight began with the cockpit settings.

Everything was already set properly for the inspection, except that the gear was raised.

She started her pocket recorder. It made a satisfying click and she could see the tape begin to spool in the microcassette.

"Crash of Mooney M201, tail number N353CV approximately eight statue miles east southeast of Trapper Mountain, Idaho. Incident date 19 September 2003 at approximately 0815 hours Mountain Standard Time." She backed up the tape and replaced the last part with "between 0815 and 0828 hours Mountain Standard Time."

She glanced inside once more through the cockpit window.

"Following preflight instructions, all systems in the cockpit are off. The gear is retracted as it was a belly landing. Proceeding to Step Two."

The second step was to inspect the instrument static air port along the starboard side of the tailcone.

She stepped off the wing onto the snow and plunged into deep powder up to her waist.

After some internal debate, Miranda turned off the pocket recorder, and backed it up to just before her sharp squeal of surprise.

4

DISCOVERING THAT THE GROUND UNDER THE DEEP SNOW WAS decidedly uneven, she'd spent the next three hours creating a proper snowy scaffolding to perform her inspection.

First she'd forged a path around the plane's perimeter. Then she'd backfilled low spots and tromped more snow into place. When she was done, it was a squared-off trench a meter wide and half a meter deep that completely encircled the plane.

With an acceptable perimeter, she began her inspection again, recording each step with her vocal notes and her new Canon EOS digital. The efficiency of skipping the steps of developing film, and scanning prints to build the sample NTSB reports she'd created, had convinced her that it was worth the ten thousand dollars for the camera.

She allowed herself a thirty-minute lunch break in the cockpit, eating the turkey sandwich she'd packed against the possibility of no food to her liking at her planned refueling stop in Rapid City, South Dakota (airport location

20

identifier RAP). As an exercise during lunch, she reviewed all of the details she could remember about RAP's approaches and runways, then double-checked them against the Jeppesen guide. Then the NTSB reports for RAP: fourteen incidents with five fatalities in the last forty years.

After lunch, other than the area of the wing under the fallen tree—which she couldn't inspect further without a saw or a come-along winch—all that remained was the engine.

Excluding everything else first had seemed to make sense when she'd first thought of it.

The snow that the tree had dumped over her airplane's nose this morning had been partially melted by the cooling engine. Now it was a hard sheen of ice over the closed and latched cowlings. Beating it with gloved fists wasn't sufficient to break free the ice.

All of her fears about the start of her new job had cost her last night's sleep. Could she do this? Or would she fail as she had at so many things most people found to be so easy?

It was her first-ever step from academia to the "real" world.

No matter how encouraging Tante Daniels declared the transition to be, Miranda could feel the overwhelm awaiting her like a microburst of wind shear ready to smash her into the ground just like the 1985 crash of Delta Airlines Flight 191 at Dallas/Fort Worth that had killed a hundred and thirty-seven people.

Unable to tolerate the sense of pending destruction, she'd changed her flight plan and departed three hours before she'd intended, well before dawn.

Per the revised plan, she should have been in Rapid City an hour ago for refueling.

However, the FAA still wouldn't be alerted. Per her filed flight plan, she intended to travel the additional two hours to Sioux City, Iowa (SUX)—three incidents, a hundred and fourteen fatalities—so that she was past halfway to DC before stopping for the night. Her flight plan would still be open until late in the afternoon. Only thirty minutes after her anticipated arrival, when she failed to close the flight plan in a timely fashion, would any search begin.

Which reminded her of a step she'd failed to make. It wouldn't be relevant until someone came looking for her, but it seemed wise to do it sooner rather than later. Per Figure 6-2-1 of the Airman's Information Manual, she created a large V on top of the airplane's fuselage with duct tape. It was the signal for "Require Assistance." With that, she went back to trying to break the ice over the engine.

However, she was exhausted. After the third time she stumbled into the propeller, she returned to the cabin for a nap.

Still fully dressed, she curled up on the narrow back seat, and pulled an emergency thermal blanket over herself. All she needed was a short nap.

Then she'd continue.

5

THE STARS WERE ETCHED BRILLIANTLY AGAINST THE SKY WHEN she woke. They were sharper up here in the mountains above twenty-one percent of the atmosphere at sixty-eight hundred feet than down on her island.

They never looked like this on a night flight, even with the instrument panel lights dimmed down. They were sharper than she'd ever seen. There were so many more stars than she was used to seeing, even from the darkness of her island home, that she had trouble finding the constellations Dad had taught her.

She hadn't learned the constellations from the Big Dipper. She'd always started with the star-outlined thrones of the king and queen—Samuel and Olivia Holmes Chase.

"And there you are, Miranda. Riding the winged horse Pegasus."

It had caused her no end of embarrassment in the only planetarium show she'd ever attended on campus. The presenter had stated that the constellations' real names were Cepheus, Cassiopeia, and Andromeda.

She'd argued with the professor in front of the whole audience until he had produced four separate texts naming it for the Greek myth rather than her family. She'd stalked out of the show and gone to the university library. No matter what text or chart she'd consulted, the professor's statement was accurate.

But that made her own father's teachings...*inaccurate.*

How was she supposed to manage that?

She'd been fifteen and a freshman at the University of Washington. Her father was two years gone by then, so she had no way to ask him what else he'd taught her that were lies.

She hadn't remembered much else after that.

Apparently she'd "corrected" over thirty-seven references —including three rare historical sky charts—before security came and escorted her out of the library despite her cries that she had to fix all of the others.

Just as she had so often in the last years of high school, Tante Daniels had attended classes with her for the next few months. Her governess had always been so kind and patient.

Miranda understood now, but she still couldn't bear to enter a planetarium.

She looked up and found Sam Chase's star-throne. The big W of Olivia Holmes' was blocked by a mountain peak, but would be coming back out soon. And there was Miranda, her home in the sky.

6

HER SECOND DAY IN THE MOUNTAINS STARTED LESS propitiously than the first.

Twenty-four hours ago, she'd already woken, showered, had a final breakfast of oatmeal and dried fruit on the island, then taken off and turned east toward the sunrise.

In the days before departure, she'd carefully apportioned all her perishables so that she'd finished the last of them during her final dinner on the island. It would be months before she returned to Spieden. For now, its lone inhabitants would be the birds, deer, and other fauna.

Last night she'd slept through dinner.

This morning's breakfast was trail mix. Perhaps it was a good thing she hadn't fed any to the Steller's Jay asking its question of, "What? What? What? What? What?"

Her water bottle was half frozen. She slipped it into the inside pocket of her jacket because she'd read that's how Arctic explorers had kept their water from turning to ice.

The morning was cloudy as she crawled out of the cabin.

Sadly out of options, she selected a hammer and used it to break the ice from the engine cowlings. It would cause additional damage that hadn't already been caused by the crash. She was careful not to look at the port side wing because she could feel its pain where the tree had pierced it multiple times.

A part of her knew that this plane would never fly again. In fact, it would probably never be recovered from this remote wilderness. In some distant future, when loggers were again harvesting this slope, they'd stumble on the wreckage and perhaps wonder what had happened here.

Yes. Making sure to answer that question for them was the correct course of action.

Still, the first blow was so difficult. This was her father's favorite plane. It had become her favorite plane.

Even hammering gently at the ice, the engine cowling was soon dimpled with dozens of dings.

By the time she had both cowlings open, a flurry of snow dusted down over the engine. She'd best hurry.

Miranda built herself a flat table of hard-beaten snow—she didn't want to have any parts she set on it falling into the depths.

She hadn't yet reached the turbine engine portion of her Aircraft Maintenance Engineer training, but they'd already covered piston engines in depth.

Stage by stage she disassembled the Lycoming IO-360 engine. First the outer layer of starter and alternator. Both turned freely, the belts were unbroken. Then she began testing the electrical system with her voltmeter.

Several times she had to return to the baggage compartment for additional tools.

The snow was becoming a problem, it kept dusting over the parts on her workbench.

Her lightweight flying jacket made an effective snow shield if she grouped the removed parts very closely on her snow bench.

By the time she was using a headlamp, she had the engine sufficiently disassembled that she finally found the problem. A failed cylinder head had allowed a significant amount of fuel to build up. The muffled bang she'd heard had been an uncontrolled explosion of the excess fuel. The piston hadn't survived. It would take a great deal of metallurgy to determine if it was a fault in the manufacture, or there had been excessive wear that hadn't been spotted in last year's overhaul.

But the root cause had been determined, and she had all of the information possible outside of a laboratory.

She could proceed with writing the report now.

7

WANTING TO BE CLEARHEADED WHEN SHE WROTE HER VERY first NTSB report, Miranda waited for the morning. Gloves were making the typing difficult, the inside of the plane was little warmer than the outside.

Her breath had created a layer of ice on the inside of the windows.

Then she noticed the battery life on her laptop. If she didn't hurry, the battery would run out before she could complete her report.

Taking off her gloves made her skin and joints ache, but she was able to type much more accurately and quickly.

NTSB reports had a clean linearity to them.

A header of basic aircraft and location information. She still fretted over the accurate time for the Date & Time block. Placing "1 None" in the Persons / Injuries field was something of a relief however.

It took her over an hour to complete the Analysis, Probable Cause and Findings, and Factual Information sections despite having stayed up much of the night composing the report in her head. The thought process had served to distract her from the cold and the growling of her stomach.

It was a technique Tante Daniels had taught her. When the input from the world had been too much and made her feel as if she was going to shatter, she'd taught Miranda to pull her focus in on a mental project to the exclusion of all else. It was using her spectrum disorder to advantage rather than the commonly perceived disadvantage.

She'd also reminded Miranda not to do that while flying or driving a car, which she had made a special note of.

Deal with the problem first.

Well, that's what she was doing.

She blew on her cupped fingers and then continued typing.

It became a heated race between failing battery power and the Pilot, Aircraft, Meteorological, and Wreckage data sections.

The pilot's door opened abruptly.

"Hey, we've got a live one," a man in a bulky, bright orange snowsuit called over his shoulder before turning back to her. "Are you okay?"

Two percent charge. She'd already cleared three Low Battery warnings.

Only one short section to go.

"Yes."

"Who are you?"

"Yes."

"What?"

She ignored him and filled in the last section:

Administrative Information. Maybe speaking what she was typing would keep him quiet for a moment.

"Investigator in Charge: Miranda Chase. Report Date: September 21, 2003." She hit Save, but didn't have a chance to close or backup the document before her laptop shut down. She could only hope that it was safe.

"How did the NTSB get here before we did? Where's the pilot?"

"I'm the pilot."

"You're the pilot?" He scratched at the side of his parka's hood.

She'd already communicated that information. The purpose of repeating information had always eluded her.

"You're the pilot and an NTSB investigator—both? You've been sitting up here in the snow investigating your own crash?"

That was also self-evident.

"Jesus, lady. Didn't you even think to brush off the snow so that we could find your plane? Your ELT battery is fading badly. Another hour we'd never have been able to trace the signal."

She checked her watch. "If it lasts that long, it will have survived for its full duty cycle of forty-eight hours." With a possible eighteen-minute differential.

"Did you think even once about saving *yourself*?"

That stopped Miranda long enough to realize that her fingers were freezing cold. She put her laptop into her flight bag and pulled on her gloves.

Save herself?

There was nothing about that in the Pilot's Operating Handbook for the Mooney 201.

There was Section 6-2-6 of the Airmen's Information Manual. It addressed search-and-rescue information, but didn't detail responsibilities of the pilot in facilitating their own rescue beyond the clear marking atop her fuselage.

"I made the V."

"The V?"

She pointed at the cockpit's ceiling.

Still outside the plane, he looked up at the roof then back down at her. "You've got a foot of fresh powder up there."

"Oh."

Miranda considered what to do next.

It took her only a few moments.

Was saving herself something Dad would do?

Yes, he'd always pushed her, but he'd also always tried to protect her.

She pulled out her personal notebook, but the ink in the pen had frozen.

She'd have to remember the note until she arrived somewhere warmer.

8

————

MIRANDA ARRIVED IN WASHINGTON, DC LESS THAN AN HOUR before the first class at the NTSB Academy. By the time she'd retrieved her baggage—there'd been rather a lot of fuss about all of the tools in her vest until she'd reluctantly agreed to check them—and visited a business center, she was only two minutes early for the first class.

The lecture hall could seat forty and about half of the seats were already full. The Academy was brand new and she could still smell the paint from the white walls. She didn't much like the fluorescent lights. They always seemed to flicker at the edge of her vision, but never straight on. Like they were teasing her and she'd never liked being teased. She'd never trusted fluorescents.

Unsure of the procedures, she'd carried her bound report to the instructor standing at the front lectern.

He was a middle-aged black man. His NTSB badge was clearly labeled Aeronautic Division and showed him smiling at the camera. Miranda, never comfortable with looking at people's faces, was glad that she didn't have to look any higher.

"Professor Terence Graham," she read his name from his badge. "I have a report to file."

"This isn't really the place."

But she didn't know what else to do with it. Perhaps *this* was the reason people repeated themselves?

She held out the printed-and-bound report. "I have a report to file." Perhaps repeating herself for emphasis was an acceptable practice?

He took it from her gently then read aloud, "Aircraft Accident Report. Mooney 201 in the Bitterroot Wilderness, Idaho. This is dated just three days ago."

It was.

"The Investigator-In-Charge is a Miranda Chase. I thought I knew all the IICs here."

"I'm Miranda Chase. I'm joining the NTSB today."

She looked up far enough to see that his mouth was set in a straight line. It wasn't an unhappy frown or a happy smile, so she was unsure how to interpret it.

He flipped through it.

"It's all there, sir: cover sheet, executive summary, the full report, thirty pages of supporting images, as well as a detailed summary of my findings of the engine. I'm sorry, I wasn't able to come up with any recommendations regarding the aircraft due to the type of failure. The rescue team only had snowmobiles, so we had no ability to extract and retrieve the engine block for further study."

He stopped, stuck his finger in between two pages, then flipped back toward the front.

"Is this accurate?"

She looked up enough to see the header information on the summary page. She could also see that no more people were filing into the room. Instead, they were all seated and watching her intently. She was also the only woman in a room of thirty men, and at twenty, she was by far the youngest.

"Yes, sir. Or I wouldn't have written it."

"You crashed in the Idaho wilderness seventy-two hours ago and then investigated your own crash?"

There was a buzz of chatter and a few laughs from the other students. The laughs didn't sound like ha-ha funny laughs. But they also didn't sound like bad-bully laughs. However, her attempts to label them didn't work: fear, surprise, bravado?

"Yes, sir. That's what the report says. I suffered an engine failure at..." she swallowed hard, "...*approximately* 0815 hours Mountain Standard Time and crashed at six thousand eight hundred and fifty-three feet." Miranda knew that this time it was only nerves that had her repeating the information that was in front of him.

He paged through it more slowly.

The noise of the class was rising, but he shushed them.

"This is a damn fine piece of work," he looked up at the class as he raised the report. "Ms. Chase has set the bar, gentlemen. With Mirrie's permission, I'll distribute copies to all of you. Other than not having been assigned an Incident Number, which I will get for you, young lady, this degree of observation, investigation, and clarity is what you're striving for on every report. Over the next six months we'll teach the rest of you how to do that."

Mirrie? She'd never much liked nicknames. Why did she need a third name when she already had two perfectly usable ones? Though Mom had three, Olivia Holmes Chase, so maybe it was okay.

She nodded her assent because she didn't know what else to do.

Then as the class again began making noises of their own, he returned to the page he'd saved with his finger.

"If you want, I'll leave this page out of the copies," he said softly enough that only she'd be able to hear it.

Miranda inspected the page entitled "Recommendations."

"Remember to save myself," she whispered it as she reread the only conclusion she'd been able to reach after the entire incident.

He didn't hurry her, which she appreciated. The rescue team had been in such a hurry to get out of the mountains before another storm blew in, that she'd barely remembered to say goodbye to her father's plane and take the key. She wouldn't have even had time for that, if they hadn't had to brush off the snow to change her V of "Require Assistance" to the LLL of "Operation Completed" so that if the Mooney 201 was found in the future, the rescue team wouldn't be called out again.

"It's useful advice, isn't it?" Deciding on including that line had kept her awake for much of the red-eye flight from Boise to Washington, DC.

"It is," he agreed. It was easy to imagine the smile that accompanied Terence Graham's soft chuckle. It would be just like the one on his ID.

"Then I think you should include that page in everyone's copies."

"You got it, Mirrie. Damn, girl, you're gonna be so good at this. Now go on and take a seat."

Miranda walked to one of the open seats.

This. This she could do.

HOLLY GAMES A NEW PATH

Holly Harper *ran away from home at fifteen and joined the Australian Army on her eighteenth birthday. She climbed to heights in Special Forces that few can achieve, male or female, until a secret mission gone wrong drove her away.*

Can a new-found friend help her piece her life together? Or is it all just a game?

1

Perth, Australia

"I'M IN BLOODY HELL."

"*The sorrows of hell compassed me about.*" Laura sassed her.

"Chapter and verse?" Holly didn't know why she bothered asking, Laura never missed.

"Psalms 18:5 and 2 Samuel 22:6. It's repeated." The game had started a couple weeks ago when she'd found out that Laura had done missionary work and still taught Bible Study groups, even wrote an impressively thoughtful column for the local paper. Holly had foolishly started teasing her, challenging Laura to have an appropriate Bible quote for everything. Laura had dared Holly to stump her and Holly could never turn down a dare. She had yet to catch Laura quoteless.

"You can't just leave me to die in peace here, can you?" Though Holly figured there were worse places to be—actually most of the places she'd been lately. She sprawled on the lounger in Laura's backyard in the shade of the deep eave and glared at the slow surf running along Swanbourne Beach. There was a time she'd belonged on this beach, had a right and a reason to be here.

"*Have the gates of death been opened unto thee?* I think not."

"Now you're just trying to goad me."

Laura stretched out in the next lounger and sipped her iced tea. "Is it working? Job 38:17, by the way."

"Not much." *Only completely.*

Gerry, the half-corgi/half-Jack Russell who was notorious for barking at air molecules, sat up from between Laura's ankles and gave a sharp yip toward the beach.

Holly tried to close her eyes but was too late; a squad of grunts ran by on the beach. They were moving light and fast, camo pants and Army-beige t-shirts in place. By their pace, it wasn't even a training run. They were knocking out a quick 10K for the fun of it.

That had been her life...until a month ago. Campbell Barracks lay only two klicks north of Laura's home. The Australian Special Air Service Regiment's base had been her home for the last nine years. Not anymore.

"Gates of death, huh? Give me a good quote about the gates being closed behind me." Holly slipped lower in the lounger. She didn't recognize any of the runners, but she didn't want them recognizing her either.

"Do you really think that you've been *driven* from the Barracks of Eden? I drive by Campbell Barracks most days, and there is no soldier with a flaming sword standing before the gate."

"No, but there might as well be." She'd left the SASR less than gracefully.

First, she'd gotten her entire team killed on a mission. The review board said it wasn't her fault but she knew better. Besides, no operator in their right mind would take on a...

"Who is it that's the symbol of really bad luck in the Bible?"

"Jonah, swallowed by a whale for not obeying God."

"Right, Holly the Jonah."

Then she'd trashed her 1974 Holden Monaro GTS; it hadn't been cherry, but damn she'd liked that car. Maybe trying to crack two hundred kilometers per hour on the beach while snockered on a stack of Foster's Lager oil cans hadn't been the best idea. It had been an awesome ride—right until she caught a wave while going a hundred and fifty kmph. She rolled the car, maybe a couple of times, and ultimately had to swim for shore as it was dragged out to sea. She'd been sufficiently well-oiled that she'd stayed loose and come away with only a bloody lip.

Finally, she'd gotten right up in the Australian Governor General's face when he'd come to lay a wreath at the memorial stone as her mates' names were added to the bronze plaque. She still wasn't sure about what.

When they let her out of lockup, she'd turned in her resignation much to everyone's relief, shouldered her duffel, and walked out the front gate. Except she'd had nowhere to go and no car to do it in.

Returning to her family was unthinkable, Holly had escaped them at sixteen and never looked back. Her friends were all on the other side of the gate, now locked behind her, or they would be if she hadn't gotten them killed in a nameless canyon by blowing up a bridge in a country she could never mention because it was all classified.

With nowhere else to go, she'd walked the two kilometers to Laura's. They weren't all that much more than acquaintances. A mate had bunged up his ankle on a run along this stretch of beach. Holly had hobbled him up to the nearest house, Laura's, to use a phone. Laura had administered ice packs, called her next-door neighbor doctor in to verify that it was just a sprain, loaned him a pair of crutches, and driven them back to base herself.

Holly had liked her, and would occasionally stop in on later runs. It wasn't much of a connection, but it was all she'd had that day she quit. And, without a single hesitation, Laura had installed her in one of her grown son's room and let her lick her wounds.

"I *know* I was driven from the Garden. No question in my mind that I fully deserved it too. I made Eve look like a rookie."

Laura was quiet for the length of half a glass of iced tea on a slow afternoon.

"Thirty days," Laura said, as if to herself.

"Yep, a month since I was expelled from Campbell Barracks and the Special Air Service Regiment." It had gone by so damn fast yet she'd swear that she could remember every agonizingly slow second of it. "How long was Moses lost in that desert?"

"Forty years."

"Bl—" Holly caught herself. It was hard switching over from speaking Army rough. Laura was never offended, but it was rude to be the only one swearing. "—imey. I don't even rate."

"Jonah was only in the whale's belly for three days and nights. You have *him* beat."

"Well, that's something. Besides, I bet I smell better afterwards."

Laura rocked her hand back and forth saying it was still up for debate.

"Bloo—min' heck."

Laura laughed in her face.

This really wasn't going well.

2

———

"'ADULT UP'? I GET THIS FROM A *COOL MOM* WHO PLAYS VIDEO games with her kids."

"No," Laura tossed several breaded fillets of barramundi onto the barbie. "The kids play video games with *me*. I was a gamer before they came along and I'm still queen of the roost."

"Maybe I'm the one to take you down." Which would be easy. Laura didn't even come up to her shoulder. Her hair was auburn and her body looked...comfortable. Holly could feel her own soldier-fitness decaying second-by-second. A SASR operator trained six to twelve hours a day —when they weren't on a mission. Missions took far more physical energy than any training could simulate. She hadn't even done a 10K run in days, never mind a half-marathon with a heavy rucksack. Laura didn't have a handy military-grade gym, though her gaming machine was a little daunting.

Laura took her time in replying, as she always did. The

second batch of fish was grilled and plated before she spoke again.

"You take me down? Not a chance."

"A challenge?" Holly grinned. And her face felt strange. How long since she'd actually smiled?

"It is so sad that I don't have time to teach you a lesson in humility." They sat down to dinner. It was just the two of them because her husband had been called out of town for a consulting gig.

However, Gerry the semi-corgi and Barney the beagle hopped up onto his chair to watch them eat. Josie "Crazy Bird" the cockatiel fluttered over to perch on the chair back to heckle the dogs from above. They appeared appropriately cowed by the foot-tall gray bird with ridiculous red circles like rouge on its yellow cheeks and a yellow ruff taller than its head.

"Why don't you have time? Sounds like you're just copping out on me." Holly picked up a piece of fish and had bit into it—when Laura started saying grace. Holly really was losing it that she couldn't seem to remember from one meal to the next that there was a grace. She nipped off the piece of fish, but didn't chew as she set the rest back on her plate. It sat there with the hot fish burning a hole straight through her tongue.

No question but Laura stretched out her normal prayer longer just to tease Holly.

When it was over, she mumbled an "Amen" and grabbed for her iced tea.

"Don't speak with your mouth full, Holly."

"Not even to bless your Lord?" Holly made a point of dribbling some tea down her chin.

"Yet another point on my 'adult up' list."

"Oh, come on. You knew I was a lost cause when you took me in."

"For one thing, I'm not Saint Jude the patron saint of lost causes. For another, you aren't even close. And beating me in a gaming environment... Well, that would surprise me no end. But I have to get ready for this weekend."

"What's going down this weekend?"

"You *are* out of it. The biggest gaming convention in Western Australia is coming to Perth."

Holly remembered being told something about that, maybe several times; then lost it in her pig's wallow of personal misery. Maybe it *was* time for her to adult up —a bit.

"With Don out of town, I have an extra ticket. You should come."

"To a gaming convention?"

"It would be a change of pace at least. We could put together a great costume for you."

"A...costume?" Holly looked down at her shorts and t-shirt. "Is there something wrong with wearing clothes?"

"Cosplay—costume play. It's for the fun of it. Half of the attendees will be in costume of some sort."

"I'll go as a soldier." And her stomach knotted so hard that she was surprised the fish she'd eaten didn't try to leap upstream. A soldier was the one thing she could never be again.

"I was thinking more Captain Marvel."

"I'm—" this time she had to swallow hard before she could continue, "I *was* a staff sergeant, not an officer."

"You're tall, with blonde hair to your shoulders, soldier-fit, and beautiful. All of that matches. Captain Marvel is about the best superheroine of them all. More powerful than most all of the superheroes too."

"Nope."

"How about Supergirl? She's—"

"*That's* a no-hoper. What are you going as? The girl ogre from *Shrek*?" It was about the only fantasy movie she'd ever seen. That and the one about that lost angelfish. Nero? Neato? Necro? Something like with a big N-O.

"I haven't started my costume yet but I was thinking of Yuna. She's a summoner and an awesome gunfighter in the old Final Fantasy X game which I always liked. She wears a kimono bottom and a top that kind of..." Laura winced and made gestures that indicated too little fabric. "Maybe not."

Holly opened her mouth but couldn't think of what to say other than, "Utterly gobsmacked, I am. You could knock me down with a dingo's breath."

"Was that some Broad?"

Holly shook her head. She'd beaten her parents' cliché-thick Broad Outback accent into the Bush and hadn't spoken it for a decade. But the surprise was too great and it had simply slipped out.

"You don't think I can pull it off?" Laura looked offended, except Laura was never offended.

"Can? I'm no longer sure what you can and can't do, Laura. That you *would* is cracking my brainpan a bit. Besides, if you went as the ogre, at least you wouldn't have to *act* the part."

Laura stuck out her tongue.

Holly did the same thing right back.

Crazy Bird Josie began to cackle with laughter, which set off Gerry barking, and finally Barney joined in with a singing-beagle howl to make it a full house of lunatics.

3

"How is it that you had this? In my size?" Holly climbed out of the car at the PCEC, the Perth Convention and Exhibition Centre. She'd been here as an Australian Defence Force recruiter many times at various conventions. The ADF knew that her looks vastly increased their enlistments and she'd been fine with that. Now she wondered if she shouldn't have been.

"I started it the moment Don was called out of town."

"Because you're evil?" Holly looked down at herself in amazement. She could stitch a wound well enough, but was better with glue or skin staples. Her outfit looked commercially done and clung like a glove.

"Because I'm incredible." Laura sounded very pleased with herself.

Holly would have to admit Laura was, simply measured by the looks she herself was getting from every male walking by. Apparently the Captain was marvelous in form-fitting blue leather with red upper panels ending above her collarbone, and a US Air Force star between her breasts. A red leather belt with little pouches that could barely hold a credit card wrapped around her waist. Gold lines accented the topography of her body. Laura had even fashioned red gaiters to cover from her calves to over her sneakers. The best were the red, fingerless gloves with gauntlets reaching almost to her elbows as if her forearms were made of fire.

"At least you didn't try to make me wear heels. I'd have had to put you down for that."

"Captain Marvel is a woman of action. Heels would be ridiculous." Laura grinned up at her through her green face make-up. She had gone for a full ogre outfit—a princess ogre right down to the gown and a tiara. She even had little tubular ears that stuck out of her swirled-up hair. She was a truly sweet and elegant ogre with a huge smile.

"So why is the captain marvelous? Other than her looks." She had no problem walking through the crowds headed for the main entrance, they parted like the Red Sea before them.

Laura had been right about the number of cosplayers. Even with her lack of interest in movies she recognized gaggles of Harry Potter house members, a conga line of kick-dancing Spidermen and women, aliens of infinite variety, and a phalanx of *Star Wars* storm troopers that she knew came from Campbell Barracks simply by the way they moved. One soldier knew another—at least at her level of training. Superheroes abounded, including many dressed as Captain Marvel. But to her eye, the costume Laura had fabricated overnight had her standing out even from them.

"Captain Marvel can fly—" Laura began.

"Not me. Well, helicopters a little; I earned my private pilot's license. But I can drive anything."

"She is hugely strong—"

"Once upon a time." Holly watched a muscle-bound guy painted Hulk-green stomp by, wearing nothing but tattered pants. They looked bloody good on him. She did wonder if he'd gone green all the way down. With all those muscles it could be fun to find out. Though green body paint smeared on her brand-new blue-and-red costume wouldn't be good.

"And she can shoot bolts of energy like lightning, but force not electricity, out of her arms like this." And Laura the pint-sized ogre held her fist out at the end of a straight arm as if she could blast aside the trio of Wookie-girls with bright pink, lime, and lavender fur. They fired back with their fake crossbow weapons that didn't even have Nerf arrows. Their ridiculous giggles pegged them as teens as no self-respecting woman would possibly laugh that way.

"Too bad I can't actually do that or I'd scorch their eyebrows."

"It's more of a smash kind of force than a burning one." Laura showed their tickets at security. She wished the guards luck checking out the vast number of swords and faux weapons, at least she hoped the massive M134 Minigun that the *Terminator* look-a-like was carrying was a fake. In her own outfit she couldn't hide a popsicle stick, which the guards seemed to both acknowledge and admire as they waved her through.

"I'd be good with blasting them too."

At the registration desk, they picked up their pre-printed name badges and she became Don—Laura's husband. While Laura asked for a reprint, Holly wondered if she'd rather not be herself. Don for a day. A stable life. A stable wife. Two grown boys. And... "Yeah, definitely change it, mate. I can't adult up *that* high."

The joker behind the desk printed out "Captain Holly Marvel" and handed it over along with various event tickets and a bag of...stuff.

"A photon blast wouldn't exactly be wasted here either," Holly showed her badge to Laura as they stepped away from the desk.

Laura's laugh was depressingly close to that of the Wookie-girls' giggles.

Once they were off to the side, Laura dug through the bag excitedly, holding up announcements, game packs, a novel based on a game, and the like, faster than Holly could focus on them.

"Look! They gave us the newest *Magic* deck. They're aggro cards. This is ace!"

Holly decided she'd better not ask and tried to make sense of their tickets.

Laura fluttered her own then stuck them in the pouch on the back of the name badge holder. "I purchased the full packages, so we can walk into any panel. There will be movie announcements with the stars, game reveals, and a lot of other fun up in the second-level Riverside Theatre. But the best part is through these doors."

Sure enough, a constant stream of people and aliens were pouring through the long sets of double doors open to the exhibition halls. They joined the flow.

4

THE NOISE LEVEL, WHICH HADN'T BEEN LOW IN THE LOBBY, became a palpable wave of excitement inside the vast hall. Any dividers that had cut the lower level of the PCEC into individual rooms at prior conventions had been folded away, creating one vast loud hall.

As far as Holly could see in all directions were booths of every shape and size. And each was crowded with people who only had two things in common: their name badges and the official canvas bag they were toting. Genus, species, hell, even planet of origin was in question everywhere she looked.

A fairy in diaphanous and revealing blue crepe with a set of plastic wings was drawing every male eye as almost nothing was hidden. A gang of steam punkers went by with weird clockwork adornments all over their Victorian garb. There was one group so odd that she had to ask about them.

"*Firefly*," Laura explained, which didn't explain anything.

The lead was a tall guy in a brown duster coat and a strange pistol on his hip that looked half Civil War and half she couldn't tell. Another carried a large-bore rifle that looked vaguely Russian and definitely an extreme work of a gunsmith's art. The three other men were oddly normal—one in a Hawaiian shirt, one who looked like Einstein but wore a collar and carried a Bible, and the third wore a Victorian suit. The women were an equally odd collection: warrior, greasy but cute mechanic with a tool belt, and a barefooted woman with a big smile and long dark hair who walked like a ballerina. The dark-eyed final woman was dressed like she'd tripped into a closet of *One Thousand and One Arabian Nights* and come out looking gorgeous. The group commanded space and applause.

"That's not the actual cast, but that they put together the whole ensemble is amazing." Laura was adding her own applause.

"Cast?" Holly prompted Laura.

Laura simply sighed. "I'll make you a list, but *Firefly* will be at the top. Your education was woefully lacking."

No, it hadn't been. Her education was the best the Australian military could provide. She could survive a month in the Outback with just a knife, rig explosives from a firecracker to leveling a city block, and shoot to kill without hesitation or a miss. It just wasn't useful in the real world in any way she could fathom.

Holly gave up trying to take it in and instead simply went with the flow, cruising through the crowds and displays in whatever direction Laura led her.

They stopped at a tall glass display case filled with plastic figurines.

"There that's Yuna, the one I was going to dress up as. And the big blond guy next to her is Tidus. They fall in love during a quest to battle and defeat the rampaging monster Sin."

Laura named off a wide variety of the other figures in the case.

When they turned to head to the next booth, there they were: Yuna and Tidus. Yuna was a beautiful Asian girl who had the body to make the most of her outfit and she easily outshone her companion. Tidus was more the pencil-neck-geek boyfriend with a blond wig than the hero warrior type. Holly wondered how long he'd be able to hold up the massive bright-blue sword that was as tall as he was—even made of plastic, he'd be lucky to last the hour but certainly not the whole weekend.

Laura sighed. "Maybe you're right. My body is no longer seventeen."

"Would you *want* to be seventeen again?" It had been one of the worst years of her life, only exceeded by everything up to fifteen, twenty-three, twenty...

Laura's smile came back. "If I could have a body like hers, maybe. But the rest of it?" She gave an ogrish shudder and then laughed as they moved on.

5

THEY FINALLY MOVED OUT OF THE PHYSICAL AND INTO THE electronic.

Massive video displays ran video game demos. Laura tried to explain the differences. Quests (with and without sorcerers), battles (from clubs and spears up to lightsabers), gore fests of violence...it all looked much the same to her.

While Laura was trying her hand at some game with swords and magic—a high-fantasy quest—Holly looked ahead to see what section was coming next. Flight simulators and aerial combat.

SASR had taught her the basics of flight. It had started with how to efficiently destroy or sabotage planes. They'd also included emergency flight lessons in case the only exfiltration route was to steal a plane or helicopter. She'd liked the helos but was far from expert. Maybe she should get a helicopter flight simulator just to see if she could push her skills ahead.

Someone behind her groaned.

Holly turned to see that Laura's player, a slinky swordswoman onscreen, had just hacked apart an even more massive knight in armor. The losing player—dressed in little more than a medallion, an impossibly massive leather jockstrap, and a sword scabbard—looked as if his world had ended. Laura was doing one of her angelic smiles as she turned to attack a charging horde of goblins. Holly watched to make sure that the real-life guy wasn't about to pull his plastic sword and attack the ogre princess half his size.

He spotted Holly watching him and finally slunk away.

Laura continued kicking onscreen butt. She'd tried to explain all of the different controls and what they did in all of the modes, but had given up when Holly's eyes crossed.

Holly turned her attention back to flight simulators in time to see a plane crash and shatter on the screen at a nearby booth. Above the game's title splashed on the banner it claimed to have *ultra-realistic crashes.*

"Horseshit!"

"What?" Laura asked without turning from her game.

"The game at one of the aerial combat booths was designed by total wankers."

"Oh," Laura's character did an impressive backflip over a troll's head, and stabbed it in the butt as she tumbled by.

Holly didn't want to distract Laura as she continued busting the other players. Instead she turned to watch the crowds, but her eye kept drifting back to the *ultra-realistic crashes.*

6

"WHAT TOTAL DIPSTICK DESIGNED THIS THING?" UNABLE TO stand it any longer, Holly had headed over to the air battle booth.

"Isn't it amazing? Look at how th—"

Holly reached out and grabbed the geek by the throat to cut him off. "Listen to my words very carefully. What total dipstick of a no-hoper wanker designed this thing?"

She eased off enough to allow him to speak. He wasted more of her time by inhaling desperately. He finally flapped a hand at five-six of built redhead. Holly stepped over as the woman closed a deal—selling a copy each to five salivating geek boys. Holly waited until they had fawned their way into the distance before confronting her.

"Who designed your 'ultra-realistic' crashes?"

"Do you like them?"

"They're total crap."

"Well, everyone's welcome to their opinion." The redhead was faultlessly pleasant, which Holly had gotten a maw-full from Laura. Except in Laura it was genuine. This redhead was more the sell-shit-to-a-cow type with an avaricious edge. Women who wielded sex like a weapon should be taken out and hamstrung.

Holly grabbed her arm and spun her about just as an American C-5 Galaxy shattered on one of the demo screens. "It doesn't break that way. The wing attachment to the main body is the strongest part of the entire plane. The shear points are in the frames immediately ahead of the wing structure, followed by forward of the tail section."

"But the—"

She jerked the now wide-eyed redhead around to face another screen. "And this? An F-35 Lightning II is a pointy diamond with the aerodynamics of a brick. It catches any one of those four points in the ground it's going to shatter into a thousand pieces—very abruptly. Even your skid factors are wrong. What friction factor did you give the ground? Hard ice? It looks like a farmer's field. At that angle of impact, wet ground might as well be glue. And this is—"

As Holly turned to drag her back to the first screen— which showed a twin-rotor Chinook helicopter lose a blade yet somehow manage to land then *blow up* on landing, which it wouldn't, rather than shredding in mid-air as it really would—someone grabbed her arm. The grab was aggressive enough that her training kicked in. Without releasing the redhead, she twisted the man's arm up behind his back hard enough to plant the big security guard's face into a keyboard.

"Really?" She looked over at the pencil-neck who'd obviously been the one to call security.

He backed out of the booth into the aisle where he

caused a Batman-and-three-Robins pileup. They'd been moving fast to show off their capes flowing in the wind. At least he was out of the way.

She released the redhead, then the security guy. "Sorry, mate. You surprised me. I wasn't hurting anyone, just giving this daft wench a lesson about reality in programming."

He tested his arm which was bigger around than one of her thighs. "Still you'll have to come with me and—" Then his eyes bulged at her. "Staff Sergeant Harper?"

She didn't recognize him.

"Corporal Jim Rankin, giving a hand for the weekend. I joined up after you were here for the Career Expo two years ago. Right over there." He pointed across the hall just as a short green ogre in a killer dress ducked under his arm.

"Can't I even leave you alone for a minute?" Laura joined the conversation.

"No. Remember, I'm not an adult."

"*Thy word is truth.* John 17:17. What's going on?"

"These crashes, they're uglier than a wart hog's fiancée."

Laura frowned at one of the screens, "I don't play flying games much."

"Well this one..." Holly spotted a black marker pen. She grabbed it and walked up to the banner, modifying it to read *Ultra-*UN*-realistic crashes.* She double underlined the *un,* then tossed the pen back to the redhead.

Attendees began pointing and laughing, attracting more attention to the booth. The redhead's face was bright red headed to purple.

Not waiting for the top of her head to blow off, Holly hooked an arm through both Laura and Sergeant Jim

Rankin's arms, escorting them out of the booth. "So, Jim, mate, how you liking the Army?"

"Liked it better when I thought you'd still be inside for me to kick ass with someday."

"Sorry, mate. Things didn't work out the way I planned either." Planned? Since when had she planned anything?

"No worries. I ended up in the West Australia Royal Engineers and I'm really happy there. Apparently they like my chops and are sending me to get an engineering degree on their coin."

It was whim, not plan, that sent her driving into the flash-flooded wash that had killed her brother. She'd walked out of the house after a final fight with her witch of a mother and caught the first bus in any direction, requiring zero-point-three seconds of planning. Army, explosives and aircraft structural specialist (especially how to apply the former to the latter most effectively), SASR...and her final ugly departure.

None of it had been planned.

None of it could be changed.

But maybe she could try thinking before whatever came next happened.

Rankin's radio squawked. "Gotta go. Nice to see you, sergeant." He saluted again, then let his grin go sideways before sauntering off. "Nice suit by the way."

Holly had to look down to remember her Captain Marvel suit. "Yet another less than marvelous moment," she muttered once Rankin was out of earshot.

"You think?" Laura used sarcasm for the first time in their acquaintance which told Holly quite how overboard she'd gone.

"Think? Not if I can help it."

"It shows," the ogre led them down a row away from the redhead furiously attempting to scribble out Holly's edit to her banner amidst sniggers of laughter.

7

HOLLY LET LAURA TAKE THE LEAD AND MOSTLY KEPT HER mouth shut.

They flipped through movie posters, play-tested games, sat in on a panel about *Final Fantasy XV* or some such. Laura practically swooned when she had her photo taken with a normal looking woman who had voiced Yuna in one of the games.

Holly arm wrestled several guys in Captain America suits that were suspiciously like her own, and always won handily. Two guys in a donkey suit followed Laura the ogre around for a while earning them lots of laughs.

They ate Space Dogs, that tasted suspiciously like a sausage banger, and drank non-alcoholic ginger beer that was quite good.

On the second day, she was waved over to another aerial combat booth.

"There's word all over the floor that a certain Captain Marvel put Adrianne down. Was that you?"

The redhead? Holly decided it was safer not to ask, and instead nodded carefully.

The guy shook her hand. "Derek. Nice to meet you. Never been a woman who deserved it more. Could you, uh, look over my game? I know I'm close on my crash scenarios, but I'd love a second eye on it."

She'd spent a pleasant couple hours with him reviewing the sequences with only minor changes, while Laura was off humbling more video swordfighters.

"That's fantastic," Derek finished off the latest of his notes. "How do you know all this?"

"Um, Army training." No Special Air Service Regiment operator would ever admit to being a member.

Derek winked. "Right-o. I was an air jockey in the Royal Australian Air Force. What you know definitely is *not* regular Army training."

Holly shrugged non-committedly.

"You know more about how aircraft break than probably any of my old mechanics, and those boys were good. You should do something with that."

"Like what? I'm done with blowing them up."

Derek didn't even blink at her admission. "Got me. If you've blown up enough of them, how about putting them together?"

Holly laughed, "Do I look like a corporate type?"

"Not even a little. I'll think on it. Can I get your number if I have more questions?" His wedding ring said that he probably meant that at face value, so she gave it to him.

8

AFTER LUNCH, LAURA LED HER TO A NEW PART OF THE HALL.
There were fewer vendor booths and far more games. The
signs labeled it *Play Centre.*

"How is this different from out there?" Holly waved back
at the exhibition floor.

"Those are new games. Just released or prototypes.
These are older games meant for playing. A chance to
compete in real life instead of online."

"No good Bible quotes about coming down to Earth to
play video games?"

"*Every creeping thing that creepeth upon the earth,* deserves
a break to just kick back and play sometimes." Another one
of her smiles, made more electric by the green of her skin.
"Genesis 1:26 among many others including Leviticus 11:41
and 43, oh, and Princess Laura H. Ware, who you may
address as Your Majesty."

"Okay, okay, Your Royal Greenness" Holly held up her up
her hands in defeat.

"You wanted a shot at me," Laura pointed toward a driving game. There was a big screen that declared *Off-Road Australia* and displayed a timer with less than a minute left. Twenty small dashboards were lined up on narrow desks in front of the screen.

"No twenty secret buttons?"

"Nope. Steering wheel, gear shift, and a floor pedal that rocks forward for gas and back for braking. Not even a clutch. Dash has speed and RPM so that you don't blow an engine."

People were filling in the seats. She and Laura grabbed the last two at the back. Her console had a picture of a piss-yellow muscle car with outsized wheels. A glance at the screen showed that she was at the back of the pack next to Laura's appropriately ogre-green car.

"I don't do driving games much—" Laura said as the start timer hit the single digits.

"Excuses already? Pretty lame-o, Your Royal Greenness." Holly twisted the steering wheel back and forth to get a feel for it. Her training had included everything from ATVs to tanks.

"—anymore. But my boys were and they learned to fear me." Laura closed the trap with a dangerous smile as the timer hit zero.

Holly eased off the line, watching for the mayhem. Sure enough. Someone in the second row swerved sideways when they overpowered their wheels. Off-road meant that they had Dakar Rally-sized engines and the torque to go with it. Two overeager cars from the third row were accelerating hard when they plowed into the spun-out vehicle. A number on the trunk of the trouble car flickered from 5 to 4, then was reset on the starting grid. Each car apparently had five lives.

She hung safely at the back of the pack through the first mile, concentrating on the feel of the steering and testing the acceleration and braking.

A wide purple arrow blinked in front of the pack and they all swung off the road and onto a wide beach. Not snockered on a half-slab of Fosters oil cans, Holly made the most of it. She edged racers down into the surf, costing many of them a car-life—too bad her Monaro GTS hadn't had more lives.

She was solidly in third, with Laura drafting her tail, when the first black cars showed up. All black, cartoon-black, without even windows. They were shaped like GT Falcons—*Mad Max's* muscle car.

"Who are they?" she whispered to Laura.

"Just who they look like, V8 Interceptors. They're the game's cars. Watch it, they play dirty."

Laura's warning was timely as one targeted her side panel. By braking sharply, the black car missed her nose by inches and plowed into the next car over.

The battle rapidly became one of life attrition. One car after another ran out of lives and was dropped from the race. The next purple arrow climbed them from the beach and launched them into a Canberra suburb (which was a hundred and twenty kilometers inland), where she'd had the satisfaction of racing through the National Rose Garden—blooms flying everywhere—before knocking several black cars into a flaming pile-up at the Old Parliament House.

The number of racers was dropping fast. The next turn dumped them into the middle of the Outback.

Six...no, now five of the twenty original cars survived. Laura was down two lives and only Holly still had all five. There were murmurs of excitement as Holly nudged a blue car with a single life off the edge of a tableland and a red one into a saltie crocodile big enough to eat a car.

"Crikey, look at her score."

Holly didn't look because she had no reference for comparison. She was being kept busy because as more and more players dropped out of the game, there were fewer left to draw the attention of the game's black cars of destruction. She lost a car-life to a simultaneous attack by three V8 Interceptors. They'd shut the gate on her before she could slip through.

She lost another when she'd tried to jump a ridge only to discover a deep lake on the far side—like there were so many of those in the deep Bush.

Laura was gone.

The hum of the other players kept building.

Back on the road, she rammed another black car into a fuel tanker that had pulled out into the middle of the lane, but the game decided she was dead as well. The flashover and explosion was incredibly realistic, as realistic as the destruction of the bridge that had killed her entire team.

She swallowed hard but managed to keep it together.

She was the last player driving.

Just as she'd been the last one standing of her entire SASR team. Caught in a drug war. Political assassination attempt.

The finish line appeared when she had only one car-life remaining. Ahead lay a narrow bridge, wide enough for a single car to enter. People were cheering around her as the black cars jostled her one way and another.

One moment, on-center.

The next, shoved to the side.

On-center...and slammed to other side.

She'd save her final maneuver for the last second. She'd have to red line the engine, and hope it held until she had crossed onto the bridge and been declared the winner. She aimed for the edge...ready to jostle to center at the last second and—

Holly stood on the brakes!

The black cars giving chase piled into her back end.

It plowed her car past the bridge entrance and off the edge of a deep canyon.

As her car and several of the blacks flew into the void—she froze.

She couldn't even inhale to scream.

At fifteen, her brother had been teaching her how to drive. Against his instruction, she'd driven into a running wash that had swept them sideways off the road. His ute, his pickup, had floated in the rushing current, washing them toward a bridge. At the last moment, he shoved her to the safety of the bridge deck before he'd died in the deep Outback canyon filled for mere hours by the massive flood.

On screen, her car hit the bottom of the canyon and exploded—very realistically. Some remote, lost part of her noted that their crash simulations were excellent.

There was a paralyzed moment of silence...then the crowd groaned out the pain she couldn't give voice to.

A game.

A stupid, bloody game and they were acting like someone had—

"What the fuck is wrong with you bloody wankers?" Holly smashed the console aside and pushed to her feet. "It's a godforsaken game! Like playing Two-up with dollar coins at a pub. Nobody died! You didn't spend seven days searching a bloody arroyo for any sign of life! You didn't blow up the bridge that killed—"

Someone was tugging on her arm. Tugging hard enough that she grabbed the hand ready to snap the arm.

Except the hand was green.

She looked up the arm into Laura's wincing face and let her go instantly.

Then she looked past Laura at all of the Supermen, Wonder Women, and space vixens watching her in silent alarm.

"Shit!" She touched Laura's arm for a moment. "Sorry. I never—" Finding no way to apologize, Captain Not-at-all-marvelous turned and headed for the door, not looking up at anyone.

THANKFULLY, LAURA HAD A LIFETIME OF PRACTICE AT KEEPING up with people who had longer legs. Still, she lost Holly once out of the exhibition rooms and into the lower hallway.

A door alarm sounded off to her left and she raced in that direction. She arrived there moments after Corporal Rankin, the security guard they'd met yesterday.

Laura caught up to him when he stopped at a door labeled, *Emergency Exit Only—alarm will sound.*

He spotted her and let her through before calling out, "She okay?"

Laura could only shrug as she raced away.

Many people were wandering along the Elizabeth Quay park that wrapped around two sides of the PCEC. But there was only one Captain Marvel, sitting on a bench by the First Contact sculpture, with her head hanging down.

Laura let herself catch her breath as she walked the last twenty meters to Holly and sat beside her. She simply waited, watching the sun glint off the five-meter tall, bright aluminum bird, standing in a small boat. The local tribe had thought the arriving Europeans were their long-lost ancestors come back from the sea. The wide Swan River was active with pleasure boats yet it was a quiet spot in the heart of the city.

The silence stretched a long while before Holly spoke without looking up.

"Well?" Holly's tone made her question clear.

"*And we know that all things work together for good to them that love God, to them who are the called according to* his *purpose.* Romans 8:28."

"You're saying that God is stupid enough to think that I'm somehow a force for good? Good thing I don't believe in her."

"It doesn't matter if you believe. And God is beyond gender."

"Because he/she/it believes in me anyway?"

"Yes, but that's not the point." For a moment Laura couldn't think of what else to say. Holly was in some terrible pain. But had shared more of it yelling at a roomful of strangers than a month of living under her roof.

Holly was having a crisis of faith. Not in God...but in herself.

Laura now knew what to say, "You have an immense power for good."

Holly looked up at her and there were tears thick in her eyes, even if they weren't running down her cheeks. Her voice cracked as she spoke, "Prove it."

"Should I go and ask Corporal Rankin how you changed his life for the better? He's standing back at that security door right now, worrying about you. Or the SASR for taking you on in the first place. I live near to Campbell Barracks and my husband often consults there. I know the vote of confidence implied by that selection. I saw it in you from the first day we met and how you cared for your hurt friend. You've given me no reason to change my opinion of you being a force for good."

"I guess I've got you fooled."

"No, I don't get fooled by people." Holly's shrug said that she knew that but it wasn't sitting comfortably.

"But what's next?" Holly asked after staring at her a long time before turning away. This time, instead of glaring at the ground, she was looking out at the river.

Laura had no easy answer. "Sometimes the answer doesn't come for years."

"Well that's freaking bonzer. You just made my day."

"Sometimes it comes sooner."

"That would be good. Really good."

There was a buzz from Holly's hip pouch. Laura knew she should have made the pouches a little bigger as she saw Holly struggling to extract her phone.

Holly looked at the message for a long time.

"You're kinda freaky sometimes, friend ogre. Someone else is arguing your point." She turned her phone so that Laura could read the short message there.

"ATSB?"

"It's from an ex-Air Force buddy," she nodded towards the convention. "Helped him out with his game design and he sends me this shit in response."

"What does it stand for?"

"I told him I was sick of destroying things."

"Including yourself?"

"Yes, Laura, including myself. But I don't think I ever would have come up with this."

"What is it?" It seemed familiar, but Laura had always been a sword-and-sorcery type.

"ATSB. The Australian Transportation Safety Board. The ATSB investigates plane crashes to save lives, instead of blowing up planes and bridges and people for the SASR for a living."

"And you'd be good at that?"

"Yeah, I probably would. I'm— I was...no, I suppose I still am a specialist in structures. Buildings, bridges," Holly swallowed hard against the rising bile at the mere mention of the word, "and especially aircraft. I know how they break and how they don't."

"That sounds good then. Doesn't it?"

Holly rubbed her at her face and noticed again the fingerless fire-red gauntlets. She was still dressed as Captain Marvel. Looking down at her body, she wondered what sort of superheroine she could be in real life.

SASR was gone. She hadn't closed that door; she'd slammed it so hard it had shattered.

Her life before that was gone. Though she didn't want to forget her brother. She'd spent years trying to forget his death at the bridge south of Tennant Creek, yet lost memories of his life along the way.

"Back with the gamers, you never mentioned you were from the Outback," Laura let her statement be a question.

"No."

"Your accent sure laid it on thick when you were raging."

Another, not so good memory. "My parents—" was all

she managed to grunt out. "I probably sounded just like my mum when she was on a tear, which was most of the time."

But there was another memory behind that one. From when she was little, her brother had always teased her with a ridiculously over-the-top Broad accent and she'd always answered in kind. It had been their language, their shared humor that created the only sliver of light in that awful house.

"Strewth? Laid it on thick, did I? Fair dinkum." She turned to face briefly toward the convention center, "Suffer, maties!" Those shallow idiots who had led such sheltered lives that they thought the game ending was as painful as losing someone.

Laura laughed with that Wookie-high giggle.

"That was another thing I lost in my past."

"*They that sow in tears shall reap in joy,*" Laura whispered. "Psalms 126. Isn't it about time you sought joy?"

"Not one of my strengths."

"Start here. Start now." Laura didn't continue.

"Chapter and verse?" Holly had come to like their little game.

"Me. Time to adult up, Holly."

"I thought that meant..." She didn't know anything anymore.

"Hey, we're two amazing grown-ups. If we don't deserve some joy, who does?"

Again Holly didn't have an answer. But she did have something she hadn't felt in a long time: hope. It was a strange, new sensation that she wasn't sure she'd ever felt before—or needed so badly.

Captain Marvel wrapped an arm around Princess Fiona's shoulders. "No one deserves it more than us superheroes."

"Strewth," Laura said with a decent Broad accent.

Holly, for the first time in years, perhaps since her brother's death, laughed.

ACKNOWLEDGMENTS

M. L. and Laura Ware have know each other for years through writing workshops. She's been a newspaper columnist and fiction writer for years (more about her works at https://laurahware.com). She is a quiet, funny, and devout woman. She has raised two boys of her own as well as an "honorary" one. She has traveled on missions and done too many years of caregiving with very few complaints.

But she showed another side while being interviewed for this story. She is also an avid gamer! She kept her two sons, and her honorary one, in check with her sword-and-sorcery gaming skills. The utterly amazing things we don't know about our friends.

Her favorite charity is Timothy Hill Ranch (https://www.timothyhill.org/) offering a Christ-centered community for troubled children and young adults. Please mention her name if you choose to add a donation to hers.

MIKE'S LAST BIG CON

Mike Munroe's *path before joining Miranda's team was all about survival. Of all the characters, he still is the best at hiding his past from others. It's time for Mike to show us who really is—or at least really was.*

1

"You're in my chair!"

"Comfortable." Massar tipped back and planted the heels of his cheap rubber-soled Rockports on the corner of Mike's desk. A pebble of asphalt stuck in the heel tread had Mike Munroe wincing.

He dropped into one of the client chairs on the wrong side of his own desk. In these chairs—cut lower, but too subtly to consciously bother the most practiced observer—Mike now sat a few crucial centimeters of perceived superiority lower than Massar. And it was Mike's job to know that perception was everything.

"Just—" he didn't know what. He could feel Agent Rob Massar's cheap FBI suit soiling his eight-thousand-dollar RECARO Sportster CS office chair, and he couldn't do a thing about it. Massar's hidden carry at the small of his back was probably carving a hole in the tight-grained black leather. Asking Massar to go easy on the furniture was like asking a Catholic priest for leniency during confession. It would only make things worse.

There was no point asking how he'd gotten past the security system, the FBI owned Mike's ass and they knew it.

This was the same way his first meeting with Massar had begun, back when the office chair was from Staples, the desk from a business bankruptcy auction, and the office was in a strip mall next to a coin laundry. Five-ten of Catholic FBI agent with a receding hairline and a well-trimmed goatee gone to gray had strolled through the front door and sat in his chair.

"Been some good years, Mike."

"Sure, ever since you horned in on my operation." Advertising had been the perfect scam. Flashy presentations, mock-up and ad placement for a steep fee—and no direct way to measure the results. When the ads didn't hit the mark, Mike would pay off a few hustler buddies to go into whatever business and be vocal about *that great ad* that had brought them through the door. Posting a few rave reviews online from untraceable accounts didn't hurt either.

"Ah, Syrian money laundering. Those were the days." Massar nodded as if sipping a Manischewitz grape wine like it was a Grand Cru Burgundy.

Mike had learned about the traditional Jewish wine at many high holidays. He might have been raised from nine on in a Catholic orphanage, but his *boyishly handsome* looks, the nuns' phrase that had initially ticked him off, had him going home with more than a few Jewish princesses over the years. He'd learned fast that there wasn't a Jewish princess alive that didn't want to throw a Catholic boy in her father's face and he'd happily offered himself. The entire race of women seemed to have serious daddy issues, which they really loved flaunting a goyim to repay. The more decent their father was, the harder they pushed Mike in his face.

Then their sisters would get in on the game of stealing him away from their siblings and... Mike never had any reasons for complaint.

He'd once asked Agent Rob Massar if he'd ever had similar experiences. They'd both survived the full twelve years of Catholic school after all, though on different coasts and Massar's hadn't been part of an orphanage.

Sure, except I was smart enough to marry one of them.

Which meant their experiences had *nothing* in common.

"Yeah, some days." Mike agreed. Always safer to agree with the FBI. Besides, they had been good, still were.

His first two clients had been a grocery store and a dog groomer. Both run by a pleasant Syrian lady who was dealing stacks of counterfeit twenties out the back door. They paid most of their suppliers in cash...he always took a check. She'd recommended him to others in need of legitimate promotion campaigns to cover clandestine businesses. His absolute discretion was his reputation. He was careful to never notice what side-business was going on.

At least not until the day Massar had showed up in his office chair, tossed down his FBI badge, and asked how Mike felt about working for the government. *We've got two fine job opportunities all picked out for you: informant, or making license plates in a federal penitentiary—completely your choice of course.*

Mike had selected Door Number One.

Massar and the FBI had guided him to bigger and bigger

targets since then. It had become a rolling client list: Client C recommending him to Client D with glowing reviews, and by the time he'd leveraged that to Client E, the FBI would be moving in on Client C with D in its sights and E none the wiser.

A rolling con, the best since he'd started dealing battered Bicycle cards in the girls' bathroom at the orphanage. He never lost in that game, and he wasn't losing now.

His fifth-floor office had a commanding view over the heart of Cherry Creek North, the fast-beating heart of Denver, Colorado's most affluent center. Fourteen miles to Centennial Airport where he kept his Beech Bonanza. The six-seater prop plane was a write-off for the company because it was perfect for entertaining clients. He loved working in advertising. Just this weekend he'd—

"You hit the jackpot this time."

"I did?"

Massar dropped his heels to the floor and leaned his elbows on the Amish walnut Mission-style desk.

Mike would have to remember to polish off the FBI cooties later.

"You aren't playing stupid with me, are you, Mike?"

For once Mike didn't know what Massar was talking about. Mike had known all about the Syrian matriarch money launderer. He'd tried a little distraction play there, but Massar had the facts so he hadn't tried hard. The FBI just hadn't had enough to pin down a conviction. Mike became their inside man—their trained monkey.

Ever since, except for the rare legitimate client who slipped in sideways, the FBI had fed him a folder first and he'd gone in with his eyes open.

No folder this time, and the current *clients* were all on track to the shitter in their neatly tiered progression.

"Seriously?" Massar squinted at him.

Mike shrugged. "I've been out of town the last few days. What did I miss?"

He'd taken the plane, his skis, and the exceptionally flexible Violetta Celeste Giovanni up to Aspen. They hadn't done much skiing, but he had a new ad account for several of Violetta's ventures. She was as well-endowed in business as she was in body.

"I should let you roast on your own spit." Massar laughed.

"The joke sounds good. Care to let me in on it?"

"No," Massar pushed to his feet. "No, I think it'll run better if you play this one straight."

"Straight?"

"You know me, Mr. Straight Arrow."

"You?" Mike would have laughed if his throat hadn't suddenly gone dry.

Massar kept speaking as he headed for the door, "We had a dog named Arrow, after that sixties animated movie *The Point*. See, my two boys loved that blue dog and named our papillon Arrow and our papillon-sheltie mix Bow. Dogs have gone and died on them, so now it seems I'm the only straight arrow. Watch out for the point." And he was out the door.

Arrow Massar had left a crease at the back of Mike's good chair. The black leather slowly filled in, as if trying to repel the FBI's presence.

"Hit the jackpot this time?" he asked. No one answered. No clue from his desk. No one sitting in the Chesterfield armchairs clustered tastefully around a low table that matched his desk, close by the bar stocked with only the finest labels. No discreet sign in the glass display cabinet filled with awards he'd never won.

What the hell had he missed?

2

A CLOSE REVIEW OF HIS OPEN FILES REVEALED NOTHING.

To clear his head, Mike considered running up the highway to Black Hawk in his BMW i8. The roadster always put on a good show for the ladies; Violetta had certainly enjoyed it. Classy Italian lady in a hot sports car was always a fine thing. But he and Violetta had only just begun, so he had no need yet to go looking for anyone else to help him warm the sheets.

Black Hawk, Colorado had a wide choice of casinos and poker tournaments where he could pocket some nice play money. When he was in a bad mood, he'd enter a low-buy-in tournament meant for beginners, play stupid, and clean up. In a good mood, he'd take on the high-level games at Bally's. Still typically ended up in the money.

Not that he needed it. Advanced Ads now boasted a very high-paying client list and the FBI covered many expenses and offered respectable finder's fees—undercover consultant contractor. Their success rate probably wasn't hurting Agent

Massar's career any, and Mike liked getting paid twice for the same work.

But tonight he needed to think, not win, so he caught a cab to the membership-only Denver Press Club downtown. The nation's oldest press club, it had a truly specialized clientele. Being in the media, or owning big blocks of it, they shared a wide variety of useful information.

He'd built any number of relationships there, even if several of them were now members of Camp George West, otherwise known as the Colorado Correctional Facility. A pair of corporate CEOs had even reached the heady status of a lifetime membership in the Englewood Federal Correction Institution for insider trading and gross tax evasion—all with Mike's invisible aid.

The FBI always came at the businesses sideways. They used Mike's information, but not wanting to blow his cover, they never revealed his role. He found the bad news, handed it off, and then moved out of the way.

But this?

Best if he played it straight?

Other than with Sister Mary Pat at the orphanage he'd never played it *straight* in his life. She'd been his parents' friend before he'd watched Mom and Dad die while trapped in the back seat of their totaled Chevy Cavalier when he was nine. She was a tough old bird and he'd never been able to get anything past Sister Mary Pat.

Mike never played it straight at the Press Club either. Instead he always played to lose just a little. It made him a welcome player in any game.

In the basement of the narrow two-story brick building, the poker room sported an exceptional bar, they were mostly reporters after all, and a half dozen hexagonal tables. Nothing fancy, just a green linen tablecloth and six players. Three of seven tables were in play when he arrived.

Caroline set his usual Talisker single malt 18-year scotch beside him shortly after he found an open seat. He only knew a few of the players at the table, who traded affable nods. No one at this table was on his and Massar's client list, which was all he cared about.

The DPC was traditional enough that Texas Hold 'Em didn't rule the tables here, instead it was dealer call. Mike didn't pay much attention as Seven-card Draw shifted to Five-card Stud and then through a round of Hold 'Em. This wasn't the sort of place where wild cards or strange variants like Badugi or Let It Ride hit the table either.

Mike kept up the easy chatter that accompanied any friendly game. When she brought him a second drink, he tossed Caroline a pair of orange fifty-dollar chips—not a lot of black hundred-dollar chips at a game like this—to let her know to stop there. She offered one of those killer smiles of hers at the big tip. He'd learned early on not to assume anything past that smile as she had two kids and a cop husband at home. But his big tip meant the other guys had to pony up more than usual and he liked helping Caroline.

The game and banter occupied very little of his thoughts.

Instead he mentally scrolled back through Advanced Ads' meteoric rise over the last five years. AA was supposed to be a quick con: run the scam for a couple years, pocket the cash, and do a quick fade. When he'd started it, he hadn't looked much past scalping the Syrian money laundress.

Because of the FBI's intervention, he'd had to expand instead of run. He made it a virtual company, careful to hire no one in the Denver area. He was the sole face of Advanced Ads and all of the invisible minions where just that, invisible. No partners. No one vying with him for the best slice of the pie. The pie was his, and the FBI's, and he was living fat on it.

Denver Post's sports editor bet a red five-dollar chip on a pair of nines he had showing but he wouldn't stop tapping his two hole cards. Big bet on nothing else.

KOA's *Morning News* host saw the red and raised with a blue tenner with crap showing. The *Post* caught himself tapping his cards more frantically, grimaced and folded. And so it went around the table.

Mike couldn't remember what he had in the hole, but saw the ten and rode out the round of bids.

After the Feds had cleaned out a Mexican drug cartel's trucking outfit, which had him running ads in the trade journals to look legit, they'd given him his first military file. He'd remembered protesting.

Hey, I'm not cleared to see this kind of thing.

Actually, you are, Massar had tossed a credit card-sized ID down on the table with Mike's face on it, a bunch of data, and an embedded chip. Instead of the FBI, it had the US Coast Guard listed over their logo. *You weren't hard to vet. No family. No close friends. A loner, and even the ones we jailed said you're trustworthy to the bone.*

Mike had picked it up carefully just in case it shot out James Bond nerve gas or something. It was definitely him, and his signature lifted from somewhere. *I'm not Coast Guard.*

Well, we didn't want someone rifling through your wallet and finding an FBI card. The encoded chip will get you where you need to go.

Massar had dropped a file on his desk. And he'd followed the recently downed Mexican trucking cartel's supply source onto Peterson Air Force Base. He offered his marketing services to help them climb the next step up the drug chain by find them a new trucking supplier—one run by undercover FBI. An entire crooked Air Force maintenance and flight crew was now visiting Leavenworth from that one.

Sitting at the Denver Press Club poker table, Mike could feel that clearance card burning like a beacon in his pocket. They'd upgraded his security twice more over the years and he was as likely now to be creating advertising for shyster military contractors as he was for Chinese tongs seeking legitimacy.

He glanced down at his pile of chips, which had grown noticeably over the last hour. The rest of the players at the table were eying him nervously.

Oh crap!

Mike flagged Caroline for a third scotch and set in to losing. But the cards were *not* in his favor. He couldn't believably fold with a pair of queens showing. Triple fours in his hand had swept the table with a full house. The next round everyone else folded when he was showing a pair of sevens even though he held nothing else.

He acted more drunk, folded when he could, and slowly bled the chips he'd won back out onto the table. He did all he could, but he'd just blown his *friendly game / easy mark* cover for a long time to come.

Of course, if Arrow Massar was on target, and he hadn't missed once in five years—and Mike had really hit some unknown jackpot—maybe he didn't need the Denver Press

Club as a resource any longer. Though he still had no clue what Massar had spotted that he'd missed.

He bled down his chips until the night cost him five hundred dollars plus the drinks and tip. He was just glad that Talisker single malt hangovers were only bad, never brutal.

3
_____

A MONTH LATER, MIKE WAS NO WISER AS VIOLETTA OOZED OUT of his bed and into the shower.

He kept a room off the back of his office: king-size bed, a luxury bath in one corner, and in the other a small but well-appointed kitchen from which he could produce an espresso, a BLT, or Julia Child's Boeuf Bourguignon with equal ease. He'd learned to cook at his mom's knee and had discovered that helping Sister Mary Pat in the orphanage's kitchen kept him clear of much of the bullying that ran rampant down the halls. For a couple years he'd dated mostly chefs just to spend time in their kitchens. Well, not only that.

He should get up and join Violetta in the shower. He could see her watching him without watching him through the glass partition and decided that today he'd simply enjoy the view. Her smile said that she knew precisely how little blood was actually reaching his brain following their morning *exercise.* She was very enthusiastic when she *exercised.*

Violetta Celeste Giovanni was a lover from the stars. It was rare to have a woman stick around this long, but they were both no-strings sorts and it worked for them. They'd spent this weekend in Aspen again. That the trails were melting and the mountain had closed under the spring's sunshine hadn't bothered them a bit. The weekend's running joke had been that they were hot enough together to have closed the mountain without the sun's help.

His Bonanza plane wasn't big, but it had an autopilot. Last night, while the May sunset sparkled off the snow-capped Rockies, they'd taken a little adventure into the Two-mile-high Club enroute back to the Mile-high City. Violetta's exceptional flexibility had come in very handy.

How the hell had he gotten here? Once he was out of the orphanage, he'd always kept it footloose and light. He still had a go-bag in a hidden compartment under the bed with two new fake IDs and a ready bundle of cash. But now he also had a plane, a sports car, a high-rent office filled with high-cost furnishings...stuff! How had he become loaded down with so much *stuff?*

Through half-slitted eyes, he watched Violetta buff down that nice ass and other delicious curves with a thick terrycloth towel. Monogrammed, no less. How had the orphan kid ended up with monogrammed towels?

He'd never been long on introspection, but if he didn't start paying attention what else was he going to acquire? A girlfriend?

Violetta, her sun-kissed skin aglow with the shower's

heat, slid over the top of the thin sheet, fitting her curves to his. "What are you thinking about so hard, lover boy?"

"You." Which was not an answer he'd meant to give. Of course, it was difficult to think of much else when her body was only a satin sheet away. He slid the sheet over her from the other side and pulled her tighter against him.

"Naughty, Mikey. I'm all clean now. No more time for play." She nipped his chin with sharp teeth.

"I'll bribe you with a salmon-roe omelet." He traced the curves of her well stair-steppered behind with his sheet-covered hands.

"You can bribe me, but I actually need your help with something."

"That's my job."

She purred briefly, left a kiss on his breastbone, and sat on the edge of the bed to get dressed. May in Aspen was not May in Denver. Yesterday's jeans and lush cashmere sweater were replaced by a flirty Marchesa strapless sundress—without a thing underneath it except Violetta Celeste Giovanni—and a black leather bolero jacket.

Yes, he *could* get to like this a lot.

"There," she slipped on sandals with straps that wound halfway up her calves. "Now my body is no longer distracting you from business."

She of course meant the exact opposite but he was far too used to such games to actually fall for them. Though he wasn't above letting her think he had. He reached out to snag her wrist, just slow enough that she had time to snatch it away.

"I have three brothers."

"We're about a month too late if that was a threat to keep my hands off you." She remained close enough to drag her back against him. Reach under that dress and nothing would be in the way. Instead he sat up and brushed his fingers through the thick curls of her mahogany hair so that it didn't hide her eyes.

She laughed. "No. They learned young that their little sister would be making her own partner choices without their interference."

"Little sisters can be dangerous." In his experience at the orphanage they were mostly afraid and hiding behind their big sisters. Out in the world, well, there'd been that whole Jewish steal-from-my-sister power dynamic that had served him well.

"But that was my love life. Now they are going after my businesses." Her voice went hot with anger.

Her businesses had put north of a hundred thousand dollars into his business this last month. It had been money well spent; he'd put his best freelancers on it. Be a pity to lose that, or her.

Scary thought! Since when did a woman matter in his life?

"How can I help?"

She leaned forward, offering him a splendid view down the front of the strapless dress, and kissed him on the nose. "You're *wonderful,* Mike. I knew I could count on you."

It took one con man to know another. It felt as if Violetta was conning him, but he couldn't see how. She'd already paid him in full for last month with an electronic funds transfer—*Business is always separate from pleasure.* Maybe it was just his old instincts triggering for no real reason. Habit.

As she deepened the kiss and he filled his hand with one

of those softly covered breasts, he decided he was just being paranoid.

When she finally rose, straightened her dress, and walked away with a finger-flicking wave, he knew what he *should* be afraid of. Mike had never before wanted to wake up this same way for more than a few mornings in a row—and they'd been together now for four weeks.

4

THAT JOY LASTED UNTIL HE'D SHOWERED, EATEN HIS OWN omelet, and returned to his office.

His desk chair was occupied. The occupant's feet were up on the burnished walnut of Mike's desk. Again.

"Hey, *Arrow*."

Massar didn't react one way or another to being nicknamed for a dead dog. "Hey yourself, Mike."

"What *good* news do you have for me today?" The sun outside the big windows was blinding and the haze blocked the view of the mountains.

Agent Massar shook his head. "Straight to business? No how are the wife and kids? Where's that notorious gift of the gab you wield so easily?"

"I sure don't waste it on an FBI agent slumming in my good chair."

"But I bet you spread it thick on that hot number who just rolled out the front door. You gotta get a life, my man."

"Sure, look at where it got you." Mike dropped into a

client chair. One of the legs squeaked. Not good for the impression he wanted to give clients.

"What part of wife and kids did you miss? They're fine by the way. Still putting up with me which is five kinds of a miracle."

"Quick! Call the Pope. You'll be sainted."

Massar snorted out a laugh. "No more likely than you."

"What would it take to make it so that I *never* have to put up with you again."

Massar wagged his finger. "Be careful of what you wish for, Michael Munroe."

"Mike. Mike Munro. Michael was what Mom called Dad. His middle name. My first is just Mike." And why had he just said any of that? He'd never talked about them even to Sister Mary Pat back when she was still alive.

"Your first name is Michelangelo, but I can keep working with Mike," Massar nodded as if he was somehow a decent guy under all the cheap attitude. "Had a father and now I am one. So I know." He hooked a thumb toward the front door. "Are there little Mikes in your future?"

"With *her*?" Mike laughed. "Not a chance. Violetta and I see eye-to-eye on how dumb an idea that would be."

"Violetta Celeste Giovanni," Massar stared at the ceiling as if one of Mike's namesake's frescos was painted across it.

Of course the FBI would know her name. Probably something to do with maintaining his security clearance.

"*Seriously* hot number."

"Weren't you just bragging about wife and kids?"

"Neither dead nor blind, Mike. Doesn't mean I'm stupid enough to touch."

"Because your wife would beat your ass."

"Damn straight. Too much to lose. But that ain't the stupid part I was talking about."

"Stupid for you isn't the same as stupid for me."

Massar looked back down from his non-existent Michelangelo. "What do you have to lose, Mike?"

"Not much. You just rolled up the Wainwright ring out at Peterson that I set up for you. Bet your bosses are pretty happy."

"Bosses are never happy about yesterday. And they're always pissed that tomorrow hasn't happened yet."

"What do you want? I don't have enough on VRTS yet. We both know that Vacation Rental Time Share Corp. is a scam, but you know I'm nowhere near trusted enough by them yet to get what you need."

"Trusted enough..." Massar was back to his ceiling fresco act. "Like you're trusting Violetta Celeste Giovanni of the million-dollar walk?"

Mike watched Massar aiming his nose at the ceiling. There was no way that Massar could know about that; Mike had barely admitted it to himself. He'd researched Violetta's business interests on Day One, and they weren't worth millions, more like tens of millions—monthly. He didn't know what the play was yet, but there was the idea that if he could pull a big enough con on her, he could clear out, retire, and be gone. No Advanced Ads. No FBI. Just him, a tropical beach, and a big fat offshore bank account.

"Keep your damn nose out of my business, Arrow."

"Hey," Massar looked down at him over the length of it. "This is a damn fine nose. Looks good on me."

"Fine. But keep it away from me."

"Just trying to help, Mike. Like I'd suggest that you take

your hot car and your sizzling lady for a ride down to Manitou Springs and the Garden of the Gods. It's the most beautiful place in the world." Massar made it sound as if there was a romance going on instead of a load of great sex.

"Go play with your trains, Arrow." Massar had revealed he was big on playing with N-gauge trains, had a whole setup at home that he'd spent years assembling.

He dropped his feet to the floor. "Whatever you say. You're the boss, boss."

Mike did his best to glare a hole through the FBI agent's back as he walked to the door.

"Just remember what I said before, be careful of what you ask for." And he was gone.

Yeah, he'd be plenty careful. He strode around his desk and powered up his computer.

Mike began checking out the three Giovanni brothers' business. Maybe he'd run a con on them. Then he and Violetta could go hit that beach together.

From snow-bunny to bikini-clad. Yeah, a damn nice image.

5

MIKE HAD NEVER BUILT A REVERSE CAMPAIGN BEFORE BUT Carlo, Marko, and Tommaso Giovanni made such easy targets. All three brothers *should* be high profile, but weren't. Nothing on them in the press. Not members of any business organizations, even the Chamber of Commerce.

Violetta fed him company names, a whole array of them, and he laid in. She wanted to put the squeeze on, then let them know it was her doing, and she wasn't going to stop until they backed off trying to take over her businesses.

He'd started it small. A rumor out in Sacramento about a deal gone south. An ad placement on the Dark Web for a hit man—by one brother on another. The contact led nowhere of course. An attack ad from a political organization that no one had never heard of and had only existed long enough to launch the ad.

Online reviews at poker sites that Carlo's casino ran jiggered slot machines that didn't pay—that just happened to be copied to the head of the Colorado Division of Gaming.

The investigation was short but nasty. An anonymous tip about mold had shut Marko's premier downtown core hotel for a week. A drug deal went south in one of Tommaso's warehouses. They never caught the dealers, but the narcos found a case of cocaine shipped in coffee grounds cracked open on the shelf that was supposed to be new desktop computers.

Violetta would come to his office in a fine Italian rage that her brothers had refused to back off their pressure on her. And the only place she found solace for her rage was ravaging Mike's body—spectacularly.

Massar had gone invisible.

No surprise meetings. No new files. No hidden notes. Six weeks of stone-cold silence as Mike used every trick to push the brothers.

Then it started getting strange.

Tommaso, whose warehouse supplied three top-security military contractors at Peterson Air Force Base, suddenly had no drug problems.

Marko's hotel had abruptly reopened. The faked mold report hadn't been proven false; it had vanished.

And when Mike had gotten curious and gone to play a poker tournament at Carlo's casino, he recognized the new CEOs that had replaced the ones the FBI sent to the Federal Penitentiary laughing at the bar with Tommaso.

What the hell *had* he stepped in?

6

"GET IN."

In all this time, Mike had never seen Rob Massar's car before. The Audi A5 Cabriolet in chocolate brown cost half as much as his own BMW i8 Roadster, but it didn't look totally diminished for sitting next to a hundred-and-twenty-grand of low sports car in the underground garage.

"Nice ride for a Fed." Even if it was ten years old.

"Personal car. I can ram a tinted-window black Chevy Suburban up your ass if you'd prefer. But I'm not actually here, so get in."

"Let's take my ride and I'll show you what a car can really do."

Massar gave him a look. It was either exasperation or *I'm about to pull my sidearm on you.*

Mike climbed in.

Massar was on the move before Mike had the door closed. He buckled in fast. The A5's wheels squealed on the concrete as Massar climbed up the garage levels, with far more speed than Mike would ever dare in his i8, and shot out into the night. He twisted through the Denver streets with all the agility of a pro driver—one with the Devil after him. Even with the i8's superior road handling, Mike wouldn't have tried half of Massar's moves.

Mike kept his mouth shut until they were five miles away, having traveled over twenty to get there, and were winding through the streets of the Highlands.

Massar eased his car up close to the Highland Tavern.

"You're not actually parking here?" Mike could feel the nerves creeping up his spine. It wasn't the *worst* neighborhood in Denver, but it had been—recently. The total crime rate had gone down mostly because so many people had left.

"They know me here. They won't mess with my car." He climbed out and headed for the tavern's door.

Mike considered the intelligence of sitting alone in a sixty-thousand-dollar car in the Highlands with the top down...and hurried to follow Massar inside. White-collar crime was one thing and that he understood. The Highlands was something else entirely.

The Highland Tavern felt as if it was one *very thin* step above a dive bar. It might be better than that, but he hadn't gone drinking this low in years. The clientele wore jeans and the ubiquitous polar fleece vests and hoodies of a Denver evening in early June. Two more weeks and it would all be t-shirts, a month until the women switched over to tube tops. Between his own sports coat and Massar's cheap suit they stood out like sore thumbs.

Massar led him to a table and a blonde waitress, who was maturing very well, arrived in a clingy black top and jeans.

"Hey Sally."

"Rob."

"My usual Bombshell pastrami on rye." He eyed Mike for a moment. "He looks like a French Dip guy to me. What do you think, Sally?"

She sized him up with the skill of a career waitress who'd assessed far too many drunks then nodded her agreement.

"So give him the Tavern Dip. A pair of Bud Lites. Thanks."

"Hey," Mike watched her walk away. He waved at the chalk board by the bar. "They've got ten beers on tap, any of which is better than a Bud."

"Shaddup, Mike."

"Besides, I've got a dinner with Violetta tonight."

Massar looked at his wristwatch, cocked his head thoughtfully as if he *was* that damned dog Arrow listening to something only he could hear, then shook his head. "And that's baseball."

"What?"

Massar looked at him. Something was going down and Mike had no more idea what it was than whatever jackpot Massar said he'd hit a couple months ago.

Sally delivered the two Bud Lites and set down a plate of tater tots. "Looked like you needed them tonight, Rob."

"Thanks, Sal." And she was gone.

Rob did look worried, which was definitely *not* normal. The guy was always cheery. Even when he was being a royal pain in Mike's ass, he was still cheery.

"Tater tots? Seriously, Arrow? I'm supposed to be eating a sixteen-ounce New York strip steak at the Buckhorn Exchange in an hour with someone a lot prettier than you."

"They're good tater tots. And prettier than me is a damn low bar that you're setting for yourself, Mike."

"What if I just walk out of here?"

"I won't stop you, but you don't want to do that. That's what I'm thinking anyway."

"Why not?"

Massar reached into his pocket and Mike braced himself. Instead of a sidearm, he pulled out his phone, unlocked it and turned it for Mike to see.

It was the burned-out remains of a Porsche Boxster 718 GTS 4. A blown aside quarter panel in the foreground was the only piece not soot black—it was the precise custom shade of green to best offset Violetta's mahogany hair.

"She wasn't in the car, but we don't know where she is. I had a tail on her even though I'd been told not to. She went into a hair salon and never came out."

"Back door?"

Massar shrugged and ate a tater tot. "Could be on the run, locked in her bedroom, or maybe she's the newest resident of some abandoned mile-deep mine shaft. This is Colorado; we have plenty of those."

Mike took a long swallow of Bud Lite to drive the bile back into his gut. It was about the only thing nasty enough to do the trick.

"Her brothers..." Mike couldn't finish the sentence.

That's when Massar's hunched shoulders finally registered. *Think, Mike.* Maybe they *had* disappeared Violetta. Just as all of the problems he'd created for them had magically gone away.

"Who the hell are those guys?"

Massar shrugged again but spoke before Mike could

threaten to shove a tater tot up his nose.

"All I know is that I'm off the case. I knew that the Giovannis were big—Colorado mafia—but I didn't know how big."

"Now he tells me. I'm from California, how was I supposed to know?"

"That's not why I was staying away. It was a good bet that they had an eye on you from the first time you touched Violetta."

"The touching was very mutual."

"I'm glad for you. Like I said, hot. The problem that neither of us knew was she was also hot like refined Uranium-238. Anyway, at first I didn't want my being around to tip them off. Thought you were smart enough to not buy into her game."

"You could have warned me."

"I didn't know," a flicker of frustration across his face was buried with another hit from his beer bottle. "I knew she was trouble but I didn't know you'd be going after the brothers, or even what that implied. Then the day after you started on the brothers, I was ordered off your case without a word of why. No contact allowed. The whole nine yards."

"Yet you're here now."

"What did I say before you climbed into my car?"

Mike had to think. "You said, *I'm not actually here.*"

"Smart man. You always were, Mike. I met you in the garage in my own car in hopes that whoever was watching would ignore me."

"Why were you pulled off the case?"

"That's one even my bosses don't know." He checked his watch again.

"What's with the—"

"Look, Mike, I'm just lowly CID, Criminal Investigation Division, the beat cop of the FBI. But I found out a little of what's happening."

"Do tell."

Massar's glare said he should keep his mouth shut and listen. "The NSB, National Security Branch—the kind of FBI heavies you do *not* want to be messing with—have been working on the brothers for years, and you stepped in the middle of it. My guess is the brothers guessed something was up even before you started hitting them."

Mike guessed. "Violetta saw they were distracted, and tried to grab some of their business, having no idea what they were into?"

Massar tipped his beer to Mike in acknowledgement. "Big brother Tommaso is a top-secret military contractor. Middle brother Marko runs the hotels where his guests, lobbyists, senators, military and the like all stay. Little brother Carlo provides their entertainment, gambling, booze, and women. Baby sister looks to have been clean. Whatever happened, the brothers used their dirty contacts to clean up the little dust storms you created."

"Just perfect."

"Like I said—"

"That's baseball," Mike spoke Massar's favorite saying in unison with the man. It didn't earn him the usual half-laugh.

"Far worse than you can imagine. Between them, they've been running a military secrets sales operation to the highest bidder. CIA twigged to it first and tonight the FBI is running them into the ground."

"All in the family, except for Violetta who wanted a slice."

Again the bottle tip to show that Mike was smart. Not half as much as Mike had thought he was, if he'd stepped in the middle of that mess.

He collapsed back into his seat. "If I *am* so darned smart, why am I here now?"

Massar kept his thoughts to himself as Sally set their plates on the table and did a bit of chit-chat.

Mike would miss Violetta. Miss her badly. But she'd lied, she'd played him. Her brothers weren't trying to hone in on her businesses, she'd been trying to grab a chunk of theirs. *Damn it!* He was *not* used to being the one who got played. She had been fun and he hoped that her lockup was comfortable and not at the end of a long fall into darkness.

But he'd been used. And that pissed him off.

Running a good con was all about knowing when to cut and run. Two could play at that game. While Massar was talking about the local high school politics with Sally, Mike texted Alejandra, a lawyer from the gym they both used. She'd been after him for a while. The tall Latina was as sexy as her name.

Evening run tomorrow? Loser buys dinner at Basta. Go dancing after.

She instantly pinged back a triple thumbs up and a line of dancing emojis as if she'd already won.

He'd make sure to lose the race so that he'd win the competition later that night.

And to hell with Violetta.

Mike dunked and bit into his sandwich. Good pastrami on a toasted Hoagie and an *au jus* that even Julia Child would find hard to complain about. After a dance on the sheets with Alejandra, he'd cash out and be gon—

Crap! He hadn't invoiced Violetta for the month yet. And running all of those dodgy digs at the brothers' businesses had cost ten to twenty times the normal rates to run. She'd promised that money was no object, so Advanced Ads had run its limit. With her gone, so was his company's cash flow —and bank accounts.

Poor planning. At least he still had his stash in the go-bag.

Sally had moved on to tend another table, Mike had eaten half his sandwich without noticing, and Massar was checking his watch again.

"What is *up* with you?"

"The National Security Branch is sweeping up the brothers and their cohorts right about now. You poked the hornet's nest hard enough that the brothers opened some cracks and the FBI and CIA is flooding in through them. A whole lot of military, congressional people, and overseas diplomatic corps are going to have a really bad night tonight. Without knowing, you uncorked a takedown bigger than all the five years you and I did together combined."

"So..." If they were all gone, then he was in the clear with no need to run. Mike tried one of the tater tots. It *was* good. Would have been better when it was warm. "That means I'm the good guy again. What's the finder's fee on this one?" Big fish paid well, and ones this size might cover Advanced Ads for months before he had to scare up new clients.

"You don't get it, Mike." Massar shook his head. "I've got no jurisdiction here. No say. I'm going against direct orders to get you well away from your office and apartment until things are done tonight."

"They were going to wrap *me* up in this?" Mike had to

struggle to not barf his tater tot onto the table.

Massar shrugged. "What I'm thinking anyway."

"Well, shit!"

Massar laughed. "First time I've ever heard you swear, Mike."

"You never met a woman as fast on the draw with a bar of soap as Sister Mary Pat."

"Doesn't surprise me. She was one of your top interviewees for your security clearance before she passed away. Believed in you hard. Nice lady."

"But tougher than nails."

"Tougher than nails." Massar raised his beer in a toast to her which made Mike feel a little better. It took a lot for a Catholic boy to like a nun, another thing they shared.

He'd never been stupid enough to love a woman since Mom had died. Better to have them like Violetta, there then gone, not depend on anyone. But he'd come close to loving Sister Mary Pat, had almost cried at the funeral.

Then Massar looked at his watch again. "They should be done by now. The whole Giovanni clan arrested. You stay off the radar and they'll probably just forget about you. You aren't a big fish, and I doubt if there are any Giovannis left on the street to come after you."

"Good news. I always wanted to be of so little consequence that no one would ever look for me."

"Ha. Ha. Ha. Look, I always liked you, Mike. But Advanced Ads is done. I've got my no-touch orders, and anything you do there will put you back on their scope."

"So what am I supposed to do now?"

Arrow Massar shrugged and at long last picked up his massive pastrami sandwich. "Have to think about that."

7

MASSAR DROPPED HIM A BLOCK FROM HIS OFFICE. IT WAS LATE, and the streets were dark and empty. Early June at two a.m. cut through the thin linen of his sports coat.

"Thanks, Arrow. I'll be seeing you."

"No, Mike. No, you won't. And Mike?"

"Yeah?"

"I wouldn't try starting your car." When Mike only blinked, Massar tapped the phone in his jacket pocket.

Mike swallowed hard, picturing the burned-out hulk of Violetta's Porsche.

Massar nodded and drove away.

Mike couldn't even wave.

Because he had nowhere else to go and no way to get there at two in the morning, Mike went up to his office. He didn't quite catch on to what was happening until he'd already walked through his open office door.

Open.

In the middle of the night.

The security alarm not blinking, it had been ripped out of the wall. Wires dangled like intestines.

Habit had him flipping the light switch before he could stop himself.

He froze with one hand on the switch and looked around carefully.

Alone.

Wreckage.

Safety and disaster mixed together to leave him paralyzed for several more seconds.

The walnut Mission desk had been flipped over. The computer monitor crushed underneath. No sign of the computer.

The client chairs had been tossed aside, coffee table shattered, the well-stocked bar for serving clients dumped— the air was thick with the stench of dark rum and juniper. The showcase of fake awards incongruously was all that remained intact.

His own chair had three neat bullet holes in it: two chest high and one head high.

There were brown, caked bloodstains on the black leather.

He managed to turn the overhead lights off again, but the streetlights shone in through the tall windows, which made everything shadowed and creepy like a half-lit Hitchcock movie *after* the crime.

Edging around the tall chairs, he made his way into the back apartment. This door was closed and it took more nerves than he knew he possessed to open it, but he did.

If he'd thought the front office and the neat grouping of

bullet holes in his favorite chair had been a horror, he'd been sorely mistaken.

His kitchen had been dumped. His machines had been tossed aside with a vengeance. They must have had a giant come in solely to kick the shit out of his espresso machine. The glass around the shower had been shattered by a spray of bullets that had chewed up the Italian tile beyond.

The bed...was bloody.

Riddled with holes.

A hand-painted silk scarf that he'd given Violetta when they'd taken a day trip to Boulder's Arts in the Park festival lay crumpled in a fold of the sheets. She'd often worn it as her only clothing when they made love.

It told him too much of what had happened.

Violetta must have *known* everything had gone bad. She'd entered the hair salon herself, leaving her car to be torched, and disappeared out the back—then come here. Arriving after he'd left to run some pre-dinner errands but been picked up by Massar. Maybe she'd showered. Maybe she'd curled up in the bed to wait for him.

The brothers, or one of their enforcers, had found her here.

He looked around and realized that the bathroom glass had been shattered by a spray of bullets that had come from the bed. She'd recognized her attackers and been ready, trying to kill them from his bed—killing his bathroom fixtures instead. They'd killed her then torn up the place.

One guy had stayed behind, sitting in his office chair and waiting for him to come back so that he could finish the job.

The three neat bullet holes in the chair had been

professional. A military sharpshooter had taken out whoever had been waiting for him.

Mike had the perfect alibi. He'd been sitting in a bar with an FBI agent and multiple witnesses when it had all been happening.

Then everything had been taken away.

Everything?

He rushed to the bed, but knew the answer even before he knelt to reach up into the darkness under the bed frame.

No go-bag. No fifty thousand dollars. No two fake identities. He was stuck being Mike Munroe. The first time he'd ever used his real name had been Advanced Ads and now he was stuck with it like a chokehold throttling him until he saw dark spots in front of his eyes.

He picked up the monogrammed towel that Violetta had tossed against the pillow so that it wouldn't get wet from her fresh-showered hair.

Mike was still carrying it, feeling the last of the dampness against his palm, as he switched off the lights and stepped once more into his office.

Nowhere else to sit, unless he wanted to curl up and go fetal on the floor. He fished out a bottle of Jack Daniels black-label bourbon—he hated Jack Black—draped the towel over the RECARO chair, and sat.

His bank accounts were close to tapped out, even if he dared touch them.

His go-bag had gone without him.

He pulled out his keys and tossed them on the upside-down desk. His office door had been smashed in and his car was likely to explode if he tried to start it.

With the FBI gone, Advanced Ads no longer existed to

any purpose. It had become one hundred percent front—except for poor Violetta.

He had a plane, but no money to fuel it and nowhere to go if he did.

Mike sat in the dark, in his eight-thousand-dollar RECARO chair with three bloody bullet holes in it, and waited.

He wondered how long he'd have to wait before someone arrived to fire a fourth round into it.

8

_____

FIVE HOURS LATER MIKE STARTED ACTUALLY HOPING SOMEONE
would come through the door and shoot him—*sooner* rather
than later. He really didn't want to have to go into his
apartment to use the bathroom. The first hints of daylight
would reveal the caked blood on his bedsheets.

Maybe he'd just pee in the corner.

Or piss himself.

Not like it mattered anymore.

When his phone rang, he almost wet himself then and
there. He dropped the unopened bottle of Jack Daniels,
which bounced on the carpet without breaking. Good. He
didn't need his pit of despair to smell like Kentucky
Bourbon.

"Advanc— This is Mike Munroe." There was no more
Advanced Ads. Just Mike.

"I'm so glad I caught you, son. Hope I didn't wake you."
The voice was deep and cheery.

"Um, no. I've been awake a while."

"Good. Good. I was told that you were the man to help me."

"I don't do that anymore."

"Do what anymore?"

"Ads. Advertising. Shilling for—" He probably shouldn't mention the FBI. "I'm done with that."

"Are you sure this is Mike Munroe?"

He tapped the video on his phone and was looking at a robust black man with hair gone gray far past the temples.

"You look like you've had a hard night, son."

"I've had better." Had he ever had worse? Other than watching his parents bleed out in the car wreck that had left him untouched or watching Sister Mary Pat get lowered into the cold ground, probably not.

"A friend said you were good with people and that you knew planes."

"Good with people?" Mike considered the question. Up until the last twelve hours he wouldn't have questioned that. By his second year at the orphanage he'd mastered the art of coaxing people to tell him their deepest secrets: Mike Munroe, everybody's friend.

Once he'd had those secrets, it had created a kind of safety. A rarity in the orphanage.

"Yes, I guess I am. And I've got a couple thousand hours and an instrument rating to fly a small plane. I have a Beech Bonanza that I'm willing to sell cheap."

The man chuckled. "Don't do much flying myself anymore. I'll tell you my problem. I've got a girl."

Mike groaned. "That's the last thing I need."

"I'm not some matchmaker, Mike, so just hush and listen. I've got a girl, I'm old enough to still call her that, who just lost her team. One person retired, another is starting maternity leave. She has challenges in dealing with people —real *interesting* challenges. Needs a go-between so that she can do what she's so very, very good at. Needs someone with Top Secret clearance too. Friend says you're the boy I want. Said you had the gift of the gab without being a soulless asshole."

"You play it straight, don't you?" And why Mike was now quoting Arrow Massar was beyond him.

"*Damn* straight! Only real way to get ahead." As if. Unless the guy was actually right? Wouldn't that just be the world's biggest irony. Mike was certainly busted now after a decade of cons.

"And what is this girl so very, very good at?" Mike could feel that stupid, useless security clearance card burning a hole in his pocket. He hadn't thought to throw it aside during the long night of sitting in a dead man's chair, clutching a bottle of bourbon like a life preserver.

"Oh, didn't introduce myself, did I? Gettin' old, Mike. Gettin' old. Must be the gray on top is leaking down into my brain." He sounded as if he enjoyed his own joke. "I'm Terrence Graham. I'm the head of training for the National Transportation Safety Board."

"The NTSB? The one who investigates plane crashes?"

"That's the one. You interested?"

"You want to hire me to be a, ah, human liaison to a prickly crash investigator for the NTSB?"

"Got it in one, Mike. Can't let her in on that though. How do you feel about being the Operations and Human-performance Investigator for her team? That's all about the people and not about the technology; don't worry, she's got the technology side wired down hard. Miranda Chase is NTSB's very best. Now, time's a-wastin'. We've got a plane down this morning and she's already enroute. What do you say? Your friend said you might want to get out of your current situation."

"My friend?"

"I'm supposed to say something about saving a Catholic brother's ass, and this time him being the bow and *you* being the arrow."

FBI Agent Rob *Arrow* Massar had just ignored his boss' orders and found Mike a back door. A crazy back door, stranger than he'd ever imagined, but still a door. Through the long night, Mike had decided that Massar's role was the only thing that had made sense in this entire Advanced Ads con. Arrow had indeed played the whole mess straight, from the first day to the last crappy Bud Lite as they'd closed the Highland Tavern.

What if Mike played it straight for once? He could hear Massar's answer: *That's what I'm thinking anyway.* He could also feel Massar laughing his ass off at Mike having to make that choice.

But it wasn't a choice at all.

"Where am I going?"

"The NTTR. The Nevada Test and Training Range north of Vegas. There's an Army jet waiting for you at Peterson Air Force Base."

"Can they hop over to pick me up at Centennial Field? I've got a plane I have to sell to a buddy there before I leave." The hangar manager had lusted after Mike's Beech Bonanza several times, which would get Mike some ready cash for when whatever this was fell through. A hundred grand cash couldn't dent his current lifestyle, but that was gone. He could skate on it for several years now if he had to.

"Then get your ass moving, son. Look forward to meeting you one of these days."

"Likewise, sir."

Mike went to hang up, but was too slow and Terrence beat him to it.

He looked around, there was nothing for him here.

Slipping into the back room, Mike kept his back to the bed as he crunched over the glass to use the toilet—which was shot to crap. He peed in the bidet. Still keeping carefully turned, he stuffed some clothes from his dresser into a knapsack. He couldn't reach the closet without facing the bed, but he didn't need any of his suits where he was going, so left them hanging.

Back in the front office, he scrounged around on the floor until he found a marker pen and an old Advanced Ads brochure. He scrawled a quick message, then pinned it down with his car keys in the middle of the upside-down desk, *Call the bomb squad before trying to start the car. Sell it to pay for the damages and outstanding rent.*

And Mike Munroe walked out the door to hail a taxi.

9

The Nevada Test and Training Range
4,625' Above Sea Level

THE EIGHT-SEAT MILITARY LEARJET WAS A SERIOUSLY SWEET ride hustling him from Denver to Vegas in seventy-five minutes. He speed-read the NTSB training manual for his *role* and had the patter down by the time they landed. He'd always learned fast.

At Creech Air Force Base in Nevada they hustled him aboard a dusty, noisy Huey helicopter with an Air Force emblem on the side panel. The scenery had a serious upgrade as it flew northeast into the desert.

The helo was airborne within seconds of his sitting down and buckling into one of the canvas seats. He could either watch the unchanging desert rush by below or the blonde fast asleep in one of the seats; other than the pilots, they were the only two aboard.

Violetta was—*had been*—the hot Italian thoroughbred type. Alejandra was the long lean darkly Latina model.

This woman was something else again. Her tight jeans were all leg. The equally tight t-shirt showing through the unzipped canvas vest revealed six-pack abs and an equally athletic chest. What he could see of her face looked good though it was partially obscured by a pleasant snarl of gold-blonde hair.

Of course, the big soldier's knife strapped to the woman's thigh should give him pause.

Pause? His lover of the last two months had been murdered in his bed last night. In revenge for her conning him, he'd set up a date for tonight in a city he'd left seven hundred miles behind. And now he was ogling a woman who even in her sleep looked as if she could kill him with a fingernail.

Shock, Mike. You're just in shock.

Sure! That explained how he'd walked away from everything a mere two hours ago. His entire life now fit in the knapsack that he'd last used for a bottle of wine and a blanket when he took Violetta down to the hot springs in Manitou Springs last week. Damn Arrow Massar for being right, the Garden of the Gods had been beautiful and it had been romantic. And now it was all gone. *Move along, Mike. Just move along.*

He rubbed at his face as the helo landed, wondering when he'd wake up to the reality of what had almost happened to him. Whenever that was, he hoped he wasn't there to witness it.

He opened his eyes but the blonde was gone as if she'd never been there. The helo's side door was open to a blast of morning heat. He stumbled out into it and blinked at the blinding sun. Where were his shades? In his car. Probably blown to smithereens by now.

Mike pulled on his best calm, which was lame as could be this morning, and looked around. Through squinted eyes, he could see that this was true desert, enough so to make eastern Colorado look lush by comparison. Shade trees were non-existent and clumps of grass only occasionally dotted the soil.

Then he saw the wreck.

When Terrence Graham had said air crash, Mike had pictured his Beech Bonanza with its nose plowed into a cornfield and the propellor all bent up.

Not so much.

This had been a massive military transport plane that had shattered across the desert floor. The fuselage had been pancaked. The two-story high nose mangled past recognition. The crumpled tail section lay a hundred meters away across a wide debris field. A single engine of the four, each as big as his former plane had been, stood like the lost statue of Ozymandias driven nose-first into the soil.

Round the decay of that colossal wreck, boundless and bare, the lone and level sands stretch far away.

There were a few people milling around the wreck, but they weren't really looking at it. Mike had been out on the military bases near Denver often enough to recognize perimeter guards when he saw them. Nobody was touching the wreck.

In the foreground stood a strange triptych. The tall blonde, shining in the sunlight like a Greek goddess, looked even better than he'd first thought. Beside her, a small brunette woman barely came up to her chin. And not two steps away, a man with a general's star on his collar was pointing a massive gun at their faces.

Mike stayed where he was, outside the leading edge of the helicopter's spinning rotor. It wound back to life and blasted him with dust as it rose and departed. The trio were far enough away that they could ignore the rotor's down-blast of wind. When Mike could finally see again and turned to look, his knapsack and another bag, probably the blonde's, sat in the dirt.

So much for getting away before the shooting began.

It looked as if the blonde was intentionally baiting the armed general. She must be a crazy piece of work to be doing that. Sure, it was distracting him from the brunette, but Mike wanted to close his eyes—he'd seen the results of enough bloodshed in the last twelve hours to last him a lifetime. He really didn't need to witness it firsthand.

But he couldn't look away.

I've got this girl, Terrence had said. *She has some real challenges communicating with people.*

That must be the smaller brunette woman. She wore a vest marked NTSB, like a fishing vest where every pocket sprouted an array of tools.

As he watched, she bent to the soil, completely ignoring the weapon. Forcing the general to stumble back a step, she pulled out a pair of needle-nose pliers from her vest and retrieved a small metal disk from the soil before waving it in his face. Then she turned to bag it. Only Mike could see how her fingers shook as she made several failed attempts before inserting it into the plastic bag.

That must be who Terrence was worried about: a woman

crazy enough, or disconnected enough, to face off an armed and red-faced general with a small disk of metallic debris. Her face was unnaturally almost as pale as the blonde's fair coloring.

A sergeant delivered some piece of paper that almost sent the general apoplectic before he snarled and strode away.

Mike eased up in time to hear the blonde introduce herself as Holly with a seriously sexy Australian accent. They looked as calm as—

"What is wrong with you two? Are you *trying* to get shot?" The disaster from his office—Violetta had left so much blood on his bed—tried to slip out from behind his state of shock. He shoved it back.

Holly arched an eyebrow at him like *he* was the one gone mad. It certainly wouldn't surprise him if she was right.

The petite brunette on the other hand ignored him completely as she carefully labeled the scrap of metal she'd bagged.

"I mean seriously. The man had a revolver."

"That's not a revolver. It's an M17; a Sig Sauer P320 to civilians. Nice upgrade from the M9 your Army boys used to carry," Holly spouted off as if any of that was in any way relevant.

"He was going to shoot you."

"Not with a revolver, he wasn't, mate. Because he didn't have one."

Mike considered kneeling down and pounding his forehead on the sandy soil. Didn't *anyone* here have a sense of self preservation?

"You're NTSB?" Mike didn't care though. He purposely

switched the blonde over to banter mode and concentrated most of his thoughts on the meek brunette. This was who Terrence Graham had sent him to help and his immediate future depended on her, not the Aussie clearly capable of handling herself—or maybe with a death wish the way she'd been teasing the general.

The brunette didn't look up at either him or Holly. In fact, now that he thought about it, she hadn't even looked directly at the general either.

Mike's banter with Holly was fun, she was sharp. But the brunette hadn't joined in. Instead she was turning back toward the wreck.

"Excuse me, is one of you Miranda Chase?"

The brunette turned back to look at him, or at least his shoulder, with narrowed eyes. Then she opened them incredibly wide—but not as if she was surprised. More as if she was seeing how wide she could make them. She didn't speak; instead she tapped her badge.

He glanced down and read her name there.

Mike held out a hand. "Hi. I'm Mike Munroe, your operations and human-performance investigator."

"You're not Evelyn," Miranda narrowed her eyes again. Was she angry that he wasn't?

He made a show of glancing down at himself. "No, I don't seem to be. At least not today."

"He *could* be an Evelyn," Holly inspected him from head-to-toe as if he was a dead fish. Usually ladies liked what they saw when they looked at him. Alejandra certainly had. Viole — He wasn't going to think about her right now.

"I'm not." He waited a moment longer before withdrawing his unshaken hand.

"Where's Evelyn?"

"I wouldn't know."

"You sure you're not Evelyn?" Holly's smile was only about one degree of separation from being a sneer. He ignored her.

Miranda pulled out her cell phone and tried to place a call.

"There's no signal out here," he sighed once more about the loss of Alejandra. He'd tried calling her from the helo to postpone, but with no luck. So he'd be standing her up in about eight hours and she wasn't the sort of woman to ever forgive that.

"Plenty of signal," Miranda said staring at her phone, "but you're right. No connectivity." Next she extracted some detection instrument from her vest.

After a few moments of tinkering, she tucked it away. "There's no signal from the black boxes. Though there is plenty of cell phone signal, I simply can't connect to it. It must be the Groom Lake encrypted network."

"Groom Lake? Like Area 51 and aliens?"

"Where the hell did you think we were, mate? The Great Barrier Reef?"

Mike continued ignoring Holly. He hadn't noticed what direction they'd flown him from Vegas. He'd climbed aboard thinking it was just another crash in the desert.

He and his dad had always kept up on Area 51. It was the thing they did together and was still some of the best memories of his childhood. Mom was always *tolerantly amused* but wanted nothing to do with *such nonsense,* so it was exclusive Dad-time for him.

He'd never really bought into it and he suspected Dad

didn't either, but it had meant that a lot of Saturday afternoons were spent on the living room couch with a couple of root beers, watching *Mystery Science Theater 3000*. They'd laughed together over the goofy comments of the host and two puppets as they watched old science fiction B-movies like *This Island Earth* and *Santa Claus Conquers the Martians*. And they never missed an episode of *The X-Files*, even when Dad finished an episode passed out on the couch —wiped out by his hours as a longshoreman.

Mike's first major crush as a kid had been Dana Scully on her search for aliens and he was still partial to smart redheads.

Miranda pulled out a satellite phone with the trademark fat antenna.

She must be calling the NTSB as she began asking questions about where her team was and completely ignoring his and Holly's presence.

He chatted up Holly, who tossed his charm back in his face, but he kept an eye on Miranda. She was somehow familiar. Like—

Renata. The memory flooded back.

The girl at orphanage who had never spoken. Screamed occasionally, but never spoken. Alternating bouts of silent watching and violent rocking. Her eyes. That had been the key, her eyes had never focused anywhere for more than an instant and not once in all the years looked directly at him. Unsure what to do with her, the priests had mostly kept her locked up. The only one she was ever calm around was Sister Mary Pat and occasionally, by association, Mike.

Autistic, Sister Mary Pat had explained one day. *She sees the world as an overwhelming whirlwind. Physical contact is a huge trigger so don't ever touch her unless she does it first.* Which might explain a much more together adult Miranda still not shaking his hand. She—

"And you?" Miranda turned to him, cutting off whatever Holly was jabbering about, which Mike could like her for. She was looking somewhere over his left shoulder. A quick glance showed there was nothing there except more grayish desert and an impossibly blue sky.

"Mike Munroe, human factors and operations specialist." Terrence had said she had communication issues and he was here to fix those. No, to *help* with those. "I'm the one who's going to go convince the general that dragging you two off to a firing squad really isn't his best option. At least not yet." He almost held his hand out again as a test to confirm his theory, but she preempted the move by turning back to the wreck without any further acknowledgement.

"Okay."

He watched her check every pocket of her vest to make sure all of her tools were in place; kinda compulsive. Then she swept up Holly and they moved toward the wreck.

Mike watched them breeze past the armed perimeter guards as if they weren't there. Perhaps she didn't see them at all. *This* was NTSB's best? How the woman had survived this long in the world was a miracle in itself. That she was *the best* at the NTSB meant that there was far more to her than met the eye.

He looked at the waves of desert heat shimmering off the wreck. A massive plane wreck. A general irritated far past reason, past anything appropriate. A general who was...*scared.* If Miranda really was autistic, she wouldn't see that. And the lovely blonde was too busy being confident to notice.

They both needed his help, badly. Mike Munroe's kind of help. Him. And for once, they needed his real skills, not some painstakingly constructed facade he kept in place for others to see. This role had possibilities, *real* possibilities. He wasn't sure he'd ever had those.

FBI Agent Rob Arrow Massar had thought this was a good chance for him to go straight. He might never see him again, had no idea how to even contact the man despite their five years' association. But this whole scenario looked just crazy enough to work, and he'd like to shake the man's hand for that.

In the meantime, he could see the general still fuming, though he'd holstered his *not a revolver*. Mike glanced one last time at the blonde and brunette as they worked their way around the edge of the wreck. Another helo arrived and a young Vietnamese kid with a massive field pack that must weight almost as much as he did went trotting over to join them.

The general stood ramrod stiff in front of his Humvee, arms crossed, and glared at them. It would be good to distract him. Cool him down.

Mike strolled over and held out a hand.

"Hi, I'm Mike Munroe."

It was time to get to work.

ACKNOWLEDGMENTS

Rob Massar has a self-proclaimed eclectic past. During the interview for this story, we rapidly discovered that we were two guys of an age with peculiar backgrounds...it made for a fast bond between us. We met through his son Alex designing the tabletop game based on the Miranda Chase book series, The Great Chase. When the Kickstarter for this happened, Rob supported the campaign at the Become a Short Story Character level, for which I am indebted to him.

His past includes: being an X-ray technician, founding a successful real estate company, and being Mr. Mom to a pair of boys. With the boys grown, he's presently the Director at Central Massachusetts Safety Council, where he oversees driving instruction for teens and motorcyclists, as well as teaching advanced defensive driving techniques for adults. He does indeed drive an A5 very expertly, and everything about the dogs is true, including the recent passing of Arrow. Something of a homebody, I transplanted him to Denver and gave him yet another role to put on his resume—being Mr. Mom to Mike.

His favorite charity is the ASPCA. You may add your donations to his at https://www.aspca.org/.

JEREMY FINDS HIS FEET

*Fans of Miranda Chase #2, Thunderbolt, may recall that **Jeremy Trahn** hadn't always walked on the straight and narrow. First he tried walking the teetering path of a computer hacker. Long before he met Miranda Chase, one woman changed his life—and one man.*

1

Pioneer Square
Seattle, Washington

"Thank you, Mr. Trahn." Lucas always called him that.
Not as if he was being formal, but rather as if using Jeremy's
first name was too mundane an action to be tolerated. "You
are a wonder."

"It was just a router block. Use that new software I
installed and it should be fine." Jeremy did his best not to
blush in front of Lucas. The man had surfed so much porn
that the service provider had shut down his user. Jeremy had
created a hidden account and permanently installed a VPN
as part of Lucas' boot-up to hide his identity in the future.

"I need inspiration for my art," Lucas waved at the
canvases stacked up against the wall.

Jeremy was unsure what *that* much porn had to do with
the strange steel-colored geometric shapes on the canvases
lined around Lucas' studio. They all looked so nearly the

same that even separated by a few feet it was hard to distinguish one from the next.

Lucas ran one a week out of his four-thousand-dollar, wide-carriage, eleven-ink, direct-to-canvas printer that was the envy of the whole building. He then nailed it to a wood frame, set it with the others—to gather successively thicker layers of dust—and returned to finding his next *inspiration.*

But part of working at The Stage Lofts Cooperative in the heart of Seattle's Pioneer Square historic district was not asking too many questions. His job, as the youngest and newest in the IT department, was to be the first-call support for artist-renters when they crashed their computers. The team in the basement of the renovated old theater building handled bandwidth, security, and a host of other services.

There was a deep divide among the renters.

A few Boomers, like Lucas, were seeking a place out of the house to indulge themselves in their retirement.

Most were part of his own Gen Z. Those self-proclaimed *visionaries* quested after something *new* and *fresh* in tiny studios—probably financed by their trust funds. Jeremy understood their work even less than he did the Lucas types.

Only a few Millennials and Gen Xers bridged the gap in the middle; the steady, working artists who actually created saleable works.

In the Lofts there was fiber art and fiber-optic art, painters and etchers, woodcarvers and writers, even a small cluster of digital animation artists gathered on the west end of the fifth floor who claimed they were making the next great anime movie. The scuttlebutt was that they were nowhere closer to finishing than they'd been three years before.

Jeremy wasn't so sure. The bits and pieces he'd seen them working on looked amazing. He wanted to argue when others put them down, but he was the only one permitted into their cloister without them first blanking all of the screens, so he kept their secrets. He wished he had some form of artistic skill so that he could join them, but he didn't.

The only thing truly consistent about each studio was the ultra-high-speed, high-reliability internet connection. The landlord made sure that fact was well known and there was never a vacancy for long.

"Buck Lucas has his babes back, young Master Jeremy?" Jack Donovan stopped him in the stairwell. The landlord might be in his seventies, but he and Jeremy always met in the stairwells. Perhaps they were the only two who used them rather than the elevators.

"Yes sir. Didn't know you were in town again."

"Not a sir, young Master Jeremy."

Jeremy had considered protesting that he wasn't a Jedi-in-training, but he liked the way it sounded much more than Lucas' Mister Trahn.

John E. *Jack* Donovan had been an Army sergeant in some forever ago time. He was still a big imposing man. It always surprised Jeremy when they stopped on a landing together as they were actually the same five-seven. But Jack *felt* five times bigger. Maybe it was the sunglasses, Jack always wore them except in the very darkest of rooms. *High photosensitivity,* he'd explained. *Even had medical authorization to wear them during formation which made the drill sergeants stark-raving nuts.*

"I worked for a living."

"Yes sir. How's your wife?" He glanced around and was relieved not to see her.

After his first wife had died, Jack had married a Lithuanian beauty half his age. Jeremy was always tongue-tied in Lyra's presence—which was just as well. She was as much of a powerhouse lawyer as Jack was a powerhouse landlord and she was always tripping Jeremy up. As far as he could tell, she did it simply for the fun of it. She made it easy to laugh along, but he never saw any of her *friendly attacks* coming.

"Fine, fine. She couldn't come with me this trip so you can start breathing again. Besides, someone had to keep Bird company." He winked.

Jeremy had learned to be specific when asking about Jack's family or he'd be as likely to get the latest photo of Bird, his pet lovebird Daisy, as he was of Lyra off on some exotic adventure with him. It always felt as if Jack was laughing *with* him. Jeremy could never quite tell what the joke was but he always felt better afterward.

"Keep up the good work, young Master Jeremy. When are you off to school?"

"Not for another two weeks, sir."

Jack nodded and didn't correct the *sir* this time. "Watch out for the ladies."

"Yes sir." Jeremy headed down the stairs as fast as he could without being rude.

He was becoming far less sure about heading to college at the end of the month.

And he couldn't help watching out for the ladies, at least one in particular.

2

———

"You deal with the dirty old man?" Penelope Nguyen called out as Jeremy returned to the basement IT office.

The room was so perfectly cliché that Jeremy couldn't imagine working anywhere else—one of the reasons he was thinking of delaying college.

The lights were dim. Any wall that wasn't covered in electronics was painted matte black. It was as if the computer screens floated in the darkness, the only true sources of light. It was half hacker-cave and half future-spaceship. From here they serviced the artist lofts as well as five other high-rise office buildings Jack owned in downtown Seattle.

And then there was the other reason to not leave for a school three thousand miles away.

Penelope was more stunning than all of the gear put together.

As ethnically pure Vietnamese as he was, she was also as culturally American. His parents were Microsoft coders and hers were Boeing engineers. If they were ever casting a movie for the perfect Viet girl, Penelope was a shoo-in. Her hair was a midnight fall to the middle of shoulder blades as narrow as the rest of her. Four inches shorter, she always seemed to be looking up at him in wonder.

"Yes. I'll cross Lucas off the call list." He pulled out his phone and opened the service app. Normally he'd have done it right away but he'd run into Jack.

"Not the dirty old man I was talking about." Penelope didn't turn away the way most girls did, dismissing him before he ever had a chance to form a cogent thought.

"You mean Jack?"

She rolled her eyes—almost manga large in her perfect face. No one could be as sweet as her eyes, but maybe she was. She always wore a black silk turtleneck that only emphasized her light skin, making her appear to be no more than hands and face in the darkened tech center. He was careful to never look directly at how the silk outlined her elegant figure.

Jeremy had never thought of Jack as a dirty old man. He'd met Lyra through a class he'd been teaching. They'd liked each other, stayed in touch, and after his first wife had passed away, they'd gotten together.

Penelope had a different read on the story. Jeremy always got this sort of thing wrong, but this time he'd bet that his view was closer to the truth.

Neither he nor Penelope had first wives to worry about, so maybe... If he could figure out how to talk to her... But he knew he never would and headed over to his own workstation without saying anything else as he marked Lucas' support ticket closed.

Between calls, they could work on anything they wanted to. As long as the entire system was maintained at top performance, Jack was a benevolent boss. If they screwed up, his retired Army sergeant side came out like a hammer blow.

Jeremy unlocked his screen and stared at this morning's problem that hadn't conveniently evaporated while he'd been upstairs: the MIT course catalog. School started in two weeks. He had to be ready to make his first choices but there were too many good options.

Should he study computer network topology or supercooled semiconductors—the macro or the micro? As for the humanities requirements, was Shakespeare any less irrelevant to his future than anthropology? Humanities had always bored him spitless.

After college he'd be joining his parents at Microsoft. His big sister was already in her third summer as an intern and had been offered a full-time position after she graduated next year. He was the black sheep for taking a summer job anywhere else.

"MIT catalog. You have some tough choices." Penelope leaned over his shoulder; her cheek so close to his he could feel her warmth. He almost cried out when her long hair brushed over his shoulder. It felt like liquid gold. No, liquid obsidian: black, thick and heavy, and impossibly smooth. Except obsidian didn't reliquefy until eleven hundred degrees Centigrade whereas her hair was cool where it brushed on the skin above his collar.

"I suppose."

"What are you going for?" She kicked over a chair and sat with their arms brushing—or at least their chair arms.

He tried to sound as if he had a clue. She listened and

made suggestions, but none of them helped with her sitting so close. Finally, his throat so dry he was afraid his next sentence would be little more than a croak, he recalled Mom's rules about politeness.

"What are *you* working on?"

"Me, and the guys," she nodded toward Andrew and Paul, "are working on a project and wondered if you wanted to help."

Andrew and Paul were the kings of Jack's system. They could tap a high-bandwidth 40G SONET trunk line as smoothly as normal people could reconfigure a home router for better performance. Then he thought of Lucas upstairs. Perhaps not *normal* people, but certainly any Microsoft brat who didn't want to be laughed out of Computer Club.

"That would be great. I'd love to help. I'm really good at helping. What are you working on? I mean do you need coding or transport layer configuration or—"

Penelope's smile told him that he was running off at the mouth. She had an amazing smile, almost as amazing as her manga eyes.

3

———

"ANDREW SAID YOU KNOW SOME OF THE ACTUAL CODE FOR Microsoft Flight Simulator?"

He was *out* with Penelope Nguyen. He wanted to take a selfie of them just so that he could check it later to prove to himself that it had really happened.

They'd taken off for lunch, walking along the Seattle waterfront to Ivar's Fish Bar on Pier 54. They'd ordered the exact same thing, two-piece fried fish, French fries, and lemonade, then taken it around to the tables along the outside of the building.

There they sat facing Puget Sound, watching tourists feed French fries to the fattest gulls anywhere along the waterfront, and looking at the boats that were parked at the Seattle Fire Station 5 on the neighboring pier.

"I've always loved the elegance of how they deal with the high nozzle water pressure when fighting a fire from a boat. You know, if they were to shoot out a straight stream of water, they couldn't shoot half as much because the pressure would try to knock the boat over. But look at how they do it. Before the pipe reaches the actual nozzle it goes around in a full loop so that it is pushing equally in all directions. Every time they aim, the water nozzle will hold its position and then they can control the stream accurately and consistently to—"

Penelope's laugh cut him off, "And I thought that *I* was the outfit's über-nerd."

Jeremy could feel the heat rise to his face. Out here in the sunshine he knew the blush would be visible, yet he was unable to suppress it. Which only made it worse.

She rested a fine-fingered hand on his arm. "It's okay, Jeremy. It takes one über-nerd to appreciate another."

Jeremy wondered if that was quantitatively true. He had so few data points from which to conjecture. The equivalency between über-nerd and computer-nerd had been a shaky proposition at Interlake High School, close to the Microsoft campus. For example, Chess Club had exhibited surprisingly few overlaps with Computer Club other than himself. It, instead, was populated with primarily math and music majors. Nancy Hammond had been the standout player, and she'd been an *English* major, further blurring the data.

Nancy was also the one who had taken Jeremy's virginity as a high school graduation present three months ago, the night before she'd left for England. She was going to travel Europe for three months before starting at Oxford. She hadn't asked if Jeremy wanted to join her for that trip, and he hadn't thought to ask himself. Had he missed something...as usual? Had she asked without asking the way girls did? Could he and Nancy be sleeping together right now in some

French hostel? No, France was only nine hours ahead, so they wouldn't be asleep yet but they could be—

He glanced at Penelope and could feel the heat on his cheeks turn into a solid burn. In the sunlight, he couldn't ignore how the thin material of her black turtleneck clung to her.

Was *Penelope* asking without asking? If so, what could, or should he do about it? What did he have to do to make her touch his arm again. He desperately needed a manual on how to be a sixteen-year-old high school grad.

Then his brain caught up and smacked him on the inside of the skull, which thankfully Penelope couldn't have seen. He could *start* by answering her question.

"Flight Simulator? I don't know it cold, but..." he shrugged. Close enough.

Mom and Dad had met while working on an early version. All these years later, they were the two most senior programmers on the project. Jeremy had learned logic structures during dinner conversations and how to code by looking over Dad's shoulder when he'd work from home. Mom had stuck with the commercial product, but Dad had shifted over and led the team for the military training simulator version.

And his admission of knowledge had worked.

Penelope smiled at him and rested that lovely hand on his arm once more. Then she offered a brilliant smile before stealing one of his French fries and tossing it to a particularly fat seagull.

4

———

JEREMY HAD SLIPPED IN SIDEWAYS TO SET HIMSELF UP.

Now, three days after their lunch together, he opened the login, keyed down his hacked identity, and was welcome.

He wanted to do a fist pump, but he knew that it always looked stupid when he tried it in the mirror at home. And with Penelope being the only other person in the basement tonight, he desperately didn't want to look stupid.

Everyone else had gone home. They were on call if something crashed that the automated recovery routines couldn't anneal but, for now, it was only the two of them.

He had double-masked their IP at the start of their run into Microsoft through two offshore server farms. Switzerland and Iceland were the most secure routes in the world for shedding his true identity and point of origin. He then added a pitifully slow connection through Poughkeepsie, New York; he didn't need speed to simply show Penelope around but he wanted to guarantee their obscurity.

On cue, Penelope had opened up an entry point in a low-priority Boeing email server with a password she didn't explain the origin of. None of its alarms would be triggered as long as they didn't touch any of the data. But their signal now passed through to the Microsoft server as coming from a legitimate business partner.

It had taken him three nights at home to build up the nerve to login on his father's computer. Once in, he'd added himself as a departmental superuser with full privileges. Then, using those privileges, he'd erased any footprint that it was his father's account that had been used in the creation. He was now *Bright_Copper_7-17*.

"Hey!" Penelope practically shouted.

"I used *Bright Copper* for Penny."

"Duh! Nobody uses that nickname. That's what my parents call me, I hate it."

Jeremy didn't know what to do. He couldn't change the username now. And he technically couldn't change the password either. He'd set it to auto-update using an algorithm he'd designed so that it would never twice be the same. No one could use the account if they didn't know his update pattern and what had been used on the previous login.

"I'm sorry. I didn't know. I just thought that—"

"What's with the 7-17?" Penny did *not* sound happy.

Jeremy hung his head and whispered, "July seventeenth. I'd been here three weeks. It was the first time you said more than hello or goodbye to me."

"And you remembered that date?" She slitted her eyes at him.

"It was a Tuesday afternoon. You had a packet of cookies

and asked if I wanted one." It sounded impossibly lame now that he'd said it aloud.

She tipped her head to study him but he couldn't meet her eyes. Instead, he watched the waterfall of her hair swing out over her shoulder, the monitor's glow caught in it like silver highlights in the flow of obsidian. He still hadn't found any other material that came close to describing its texture.

"You're sweet, Jeremy," she leaned in and kissed him on the cheek. "I guess I'll have to bring cookies more often."

"Okay." *Dumb* answer. But it was too late to take it back now. He sighed quietly to himself. Why couldn't he *ever* be smart around a pretty girl? Or around any girl?

To hide the burn spot her lips had left on his skin, he turned to the monitor and began showing Penelope around the programmatic structure of the military's version of Flight Simulator.

Her questions quickly took them deeper.

The commercial version allowed for control of a simulated airplane from the rudder pedals to the autopilot. A user could fly a Cessna through the concrete canyons of New York City, or try to land a 737 in the midst of a Dallas thunderstorm with a failed engine and no landing gear.

"Too bad we don't have a military simulator here. They offer an almost full-enclosure experience. The video wraps around so that the visual is exactly what you could see from the plane whether it's an F-16 fighter jet or a C-130 Hercules transport."

"Could this block of code here be an entry point to take over a simulator's control from the pilot?" She rested her hand on his arm again in her excitement—and left it there.

"Good eye. Yes, if we were to slice in here directly below

the primary display module, we'd gain access to what they're seeing both visually and on the instrument displays. And here—" he jumped over to another section of the code, "— we could grab their control inputs from the joysticks, throttles, even the navigation computer, and convert them however we wanted to."

She nodded, swirling her liquid hair forward and back. "We'd have to back loop the control feedback pressure emulators as well to keep them fooled."

He and Nancy had *never* talked like this. They had overlapped on chess, but not much else. Together they'd achieved an asynchronous communications protocol at best, except for a few particularly memorable moments of high synchronicity.

He and Penelope were like a full-lock SSL—a secure socket layer security protocol—with ten-twenty-four-bit encryption.

"Uh," he considered the code stack for a moment. "Yeah, that would do it."

"That's so slick."

"My dad's code." He knew Dad was good, but he liked hearing that coming from someone as skilled as Penelope. She was beautiful, a red-hot programmer, and he loved the light touch of her fingers drawing absentminded circles on his arm.

"What would it take to use this to take over a real plane? I guess it can't be done, can it?"

She slid her fingers away and began collecting her things to go home for the night.

5

It took Jeremy a week.

Several nights he didn't waste time going home. All he had to tell his parents was that he was trying to crack a block of code to fix something at work. They were both programmers and understood how consuming that could be.

When he couldn't see well enough to even count the logic nesting parentheses anymore, he'd nap for a few hours under his desk. But the code always woke him long before anyone else came to work.

Penelope brought him treats: a massive chocolate chip cookie the size of his head, a bag of chocolate-coated pretzels, and one of those bulk containers of red licorice.

Andrew and sometimes even Paul fielded the support calls that had been his all summer.

It took Jeremy a day to find the Air Force Agency for Modeling and Simulations' Cray supercomputer at Eglin Air Force Base. It would have taken an hour if he'd been willing to relink to his dad's account. Of course he would have a direct link to the AFAMS. Dad needed to collect usage and user data to keep improving the product.

But Jeremy hadn't dared follow that; he wanted no traceable pingbacks.

Two days later he managed to locate an entry from the simulations mainframe into the Air Force Combat Command's Cray where all of the real-world flight status updates were gathered and processed.

The rest of the week he'd spent unraveling the interface functionality and building his own link code from scratch. These days a military jet was more computer than aircraft in many ways.

By the end of the week he could select most airborne military aircraft, enter through the secondary data bus backbone, and take over the command-and-control for instrumentation, and even weapons. All in the real world, not merely the simulators.

"The last is the most interesting," he showed Penelope as she came to sit with him that evening. "Because everything, except the backup compass and sometimes the artificial horizon is now electronic. It means that I can show the pilot one thing while his plane is actually doing another. If it's fly-by-wire instead of mechanical linkage to the control surfaces, I can even create what he or she feels."

To prove it, he reached into a C-5 Galaxy cargo jet in transit from Ramstein Air Force Base in Germany to Dover in the Delaware. He set up two instrument displays.

"That's the real one," he pointed at the left monitor. "And this is what they see."

He banked the plane very slightly and turned it ten full

degrees off course, then turned it again until it was on its original course. The pilot's instruments didn't show a thing.

"That's *amazing*, Jeremy." Penelope threw her arms around his neck and kissed him.

He wasn't the only one who was amazing. Her kiss seared into his system like a polymorphic virus that shaped itself to his dreams and marked him to the core of his code. It was everything he'd ever imagined and so much more. He now understood that while Nancy had been sweet, Penelope would be incredible—if they got that far.

When she stopped the kiss, it was as if his world had crashed down upon him. The week of sustained effort with only brief snatches of rest, his anxiety to impress Penelope, his unfinished decisions about going to MIT next week, and everything else slammed into him and his head spun with vertigo.

"We had no idea you were so good. Tomorrow evening you just *have* to show Andrew and Paul how you did it. They'll be so impressed."

"Sure. Okay. Once I get some sleep."

She kissed him again after whispering against his lips, "It's the sexiest code I've ever seen."

He hadn't thought about following Nancy to Europe. But this time he'd stick with the girl and MIT could go fish.

6

JEREMY DARED GREATLY WHEN HE PLACED HIS HANDS ON HER waist as she kissed him goodnight before she slid into her car. A Mini Cooper S convertible. It was as sporty and had as much energy as the woman who drove it.

Once she had left, with a cheery double-tap of her brake lights, his car was the only one left in the Occidental Avenue parking lot. Before he could open the door, a gloss-black classic Corvette Stingray convertible pulled up so close that he had to lie against his Toyota Prius' driver's door to avoid being squished.

The top was down. Jack Donovan rested an arm on the windowsill and looked up at him.

"Young Master Jeremy."

"Good evening, sir. The 1965. Nice car." It was easily identifiable by the optional dual side exhaust pipes that ran below the driver's door,

"It's oh-three-hundred, boy. You left evening behind

somewhere in the fast lane. And I've got to have me a nice car if I want to drive my lady around in style."

Jeremy fumbled for his phone to doublecheck though he didn't know why. It *was* three in the morning, no wonder he couldn't stand up straight.

"Get in."

"My car..." he waved vaguely at the only thing supporting him.

"Will still be there in the morning. I fear that if you get in it tonight, you may not make it home intact. Get in, I'll drive you. You can use some of your hard-earned overtime pay to afford a taxi tomorrow morning."

Out of options, and with too little space to open his car door without dinging the Corvette's side panel, he scooted out of the narrow gap, circled around, and climbed into Jack's passenger seat.

"I, uh, haven't been working overtime." He eased down into the deep bucket seat and could feel the kinks of all the hours he'd hunched over a keyboard let go one by one. "In fact, I shouldn't be claiming any hours this week."

Jack drove them slowly through the quiet city, then turned onto Cherry Street and began climbing the steep hill up to I-5. At a stoplight in the middle of the slope, he felt as if he was more lying in his seat than sitting in it—the angle steep enough to give the impression of being in a rocket ship ready for takeoff.

"Where are you heading, young Master Jeremy?"

He thought of Penelope's waist beneath his palms as she'd kissed him goodnight, or technically good morning. He though of MIT, lurking three thousand miles over the horizon straight ahead. He looked up and saw the half moon high alongside the seventy-six-story tower of the Columbia Center.

"The Moon."

Jack chuckled as the light turned green and the big fuel-injected engine roared to life and hurtled them upwards. A block later, they plunged into a tunnel and began burrowing their way north out of Seattle.

"And when is a moon not a moon, Jeremy?"

"Well, in approximately two billion years, the Moon will have drifted far enough away that the center of mass of the Earth-Moon system will be out past the Earth's surface. After that, it won't be a moon, it will be a double-planet."

Jeremy heard the silence that was one of Jack's many forms of laughter.

"Except that's not what you meant."

"Can't say it was, but I'd missed that detail. I don't often worry about a few billion years away. I focus on the here and now."

"No. You don't."

Jack looked over at him.

Jeremy pointed at his bracelet. "Isn't that a POW/MIA bracelet?" Jeremy knew it was.

"It is," Jack said carefully.

"I looked them up. While I was looking, I spotted your name. You're the one who made such a fuss that the Secretary of the Armed Services authorized it as the only allowable wrist jewelry other than a watch and a medical alert bracelet."

"That was me."

"The past," Jeremy lay his head back and allowed the car's motion to rock him.

"You're like...twelve. You don't know anything."

"I'm sixteen."

"Trust me, kid, you don't know anything. And you're not going to find anything more the way you're going."

Jeremy kept his mouth shut. The way he was going? He wasn't going anywhere; he'd stay in Seattle and... What?

He and Penelope would...

She was nineteen and utterly perfect. Next to her? He was nothing.

But he had no idea what that meant about where he was or wasn't going.

7

"I'll tell you a story, Young Master Jeremy."

Jeremy shook himself awake. They weren't crossing the 520 floating bridge.

Instead they were *looking* at the bridge that stretched across Lake Washington. The lake bounded Seattle for twenty-five miles along the eastern side just as Puget Sound did on the western one. The floating bridge itself lay stretched out across the lake like a compass needle in the night, connecting Seattle with Bellevue and Redmond where Microsoft and home lay.

He estimated the angle and distance as well as he could in the darkness. Based on those, their low angle of elevation to the bridge, and the sparse lights on the far shore, he calculated that they must be in the park at the end of the Madison Park neighborhood.

Then he looked out his side window and stared at the sign, *Madison Park North Beach.*

Yeah, that's where they were. The dashboard was as dark

as the night outside and he was too tired to dig out the phone he was sitting on to check the time.

Dark. That's what time it was.

"A...story?"

"I've seen a lot of things in my time, young Master Jeremy. My best friend was killed on his first day in Vietnam. Plenty of guys from my high school class never came home. My job was in electronic intelligence analysis, Top Secret clearance and all that. We were the Number One intel unit in 'Nam. I picked a lot of targets out of that intel. If I did it right, I put down a lot, and I mean a *lot* of bad guys. One mistake and it was our boys who paid. Then I started seeing far too much else in that intel. Once I know something, I've got to play it straight. Started asking questions that got me eased out of the war plenty fast once I asked them."

The moonlight picked out Jack's knuckles wrapped tight around the bright wooden steering wheel.

"You like planes, Jeremy." His voice was tight.

"Yes, sir. Never flown in them but they're the most amazing machines, except maybe a spaceship, that we've ever built."

"Never flown?"

"No sir." Jeremy tried to imagine the things Jack had seen and couldn't.

"Imagine you're the only person on an entire Hercules C-130 Hercules other than the flight crew."

"Uh, okay."

"Now imagine that the entire cargo is bodies of the dead being airlifted back to the states."

Jeremy couldn't breathe.

"Now think about living with those kinds of memories every day."

All Jeremy could hear was his heart beating so loud he wondered if it could break his eardrums from the inside.

"Now let me repeat my earlier question."

His parents had been born in Vietnam, a part of the famous Operation Babylift. Never knowing if they were actually orphans or not, they arrived and were adopted in the US. Chance had led them separately to Microsoft and the Flight Simulator program. Or perhaps it hadn't been mere chance. They'd been evacuated by air to the US, one on a 747 and the other on a C-5A Galaxy. The same plane he'd taken over briefly to impress Penelope.

"Where are you going, young Master Jeremy?"

To *impress* Penelope?

Jeremy sat on his hands to stop them from shaking as he stared out at the bridge lights.

Why did she want to control a military plane anyway? Hacker cred? That would be his to claim, wouldn't it? Or was it something else...something worse?

He knew hacker games. Might they crash a plane simply because they could?

What *had* he done?

And worst of all, what had he done without *thinking*.

8

───────

Jeremy figured he'd never sleep again.

It was dark when he closed his eyes trying to block out the eager look in Penelope's eyes. And the haunted one in Jack Donovan's.

He opened his eyes to near darkness. Sunrise would be happening soon.

Ten o'clock. It shouldn't still be dark.

He looked out his bedroom window at the deep orange bleeding out of the summer sky. Sunset. He'd slept sixteen hours straight through since Jack had dropped him off.

His phone pinged as he stumbled out of the shower and pulled on fresh clothes.

There was a cute smile photo from Penelope followed by *Coming in tonight?* The message had arrived minutes ago, probably what had woken him. Now it showed a frowny emoji.

He was about to answer that he'd overslept when there was another ping.

It was from his password alert system.

Bright_Copper_7-17 had just attempted to log in to the Microsoft servers. His alert captured the IP address. He didn't recognize it, but he'd wager he knew its well-masked point of origin: the Stage Lofts basement in Pioneer Square, Seattle. It also showed the password that had been keystroked in—yesterday's password.

Except Penelope hadn't been looking his direction when he'd keyed it in and he'd been careful to mask his finger movements anyway. It was a habit from high school Computer Club. Ricky Rudd had made Jeremy his own personal target, which had taught Jeremy a great deal about security.

A keylogger. Penelope had setup a keylogger on his computer and she'd done it well or he would have noticed.

Another login attempt pinged in, this time using the previous day's password.

She'd been keylogging him for a while. Or had it been Andrew or Paul? Was she with one of them even though she'd kissed him?

Thank goodness he wasn't dumb enough to make his password pattern shift in any predictable fashion.

Jeremy looked out his bedroom window at the last threads of the sunset.

A jet climbing out of Sea-Tac was a tiny black dot until it climbed high enough to catch a final spark of sunlight from over the horizon.

Dad had often talked of the plane that had departed Saigon ahead of his, not that he remembered it as he'd only been two at the time. The prior C-5A Galaxy, the biggest cargo jet in US military history, had lifted out of Saigon with over three hundred evacuees aboard. Twelve minutes later there was an explosive decompression. Circling back, the crippled plane crashed into a rice paddy just shy of the airport. Half the people aboard were killed. Seventy-eight of them were orphan children. Dad said it wasn't about luck or fate; he just cared about making pilots and planes safer.

Jeremy looked down at the pings to his phone: two login attempts, the great photo from Penelope, and the frowny emoji.

Most systems allowed three failed password attempts before locking down hard.

As a high school project, he'd built a more elaborate response for a third failed login attempt.

Should he warn her not to try?

Jeremy didn't type anything.

His login tracker pinged once more.

9

"I'M SO SORRY, MR. DONOVAN."

They stood alone in the basement server room of the Stage Lofts Cooperative.

It all looked so normal. He could see the status screen rolling as various users logged in and accessed their data.

He looked around, but the other three IT staff were gone, the FBI had taken them away. So were the machines that the other admins had been using—fifty thousand dollars of top gear.

At Interlake High School Computer Club, his data protection application had inspected who had logged onto the machine being used to attempt to break Jeremy's encrypted login. At the third failed attempt, it had grabbed all of Ricky Rudd's user information using the open password in the background. Every single piece of which had then been published as a school-wide email. He'd been a bully and an abusive troll. No longer safely anonymous, the exposé had been so bad that his parents had quietly left Microsoft and moved out of the area.

This time, his app had scraped Penelope's entire master user account and sent it to him. Jeremy had seen what was in it. A lot of Black Hat hacker crap. Boeing designs that had classified stamped on them had only been the beginning. She and the others were hackers of the worst type—virus designs, military level hacking tools, and way more he'd never wanted to know about.

Out of ideas about what he could possibly do, he had the computer post it anonymously to Jack.

Jack had called him and only asked one word, "You?"

Jeremy had replied, "Playing it straight."

Jack had hung up.

He'd then forwarded it to the FBI.

Any traces of his hack of Microsoft and the Flight Simulator had been under his own username. At Jack's insistence he'd said that he'd been showing Penelope a fake simulation that had taken him all week to build as a trap. He wasn't comfortable lying to the FBI, but neither was he comfortable having to tell his parents and them giving up their life's dream as Ricky Rudd's parents had.

For three days after Paul, Andrew, and Penelope were arrested, he and Jack Donovan had been interviewed for endless hours. But he'd ended up with no record, and his parents had never found out what he'd almost done.

Half the gear was gone and the entire support staff except for himself.

"I'm so sorry, Mr. Donovan. I thought I knew what was happening."

"You stepped up when it mattered."

"But..." he waved a hand helplessly at the mess.

"Never, for the sake of peace and quiet, deny your own experience or conviction. I've always liked that quote. This time you didn't get the girl—but you didn't lose yourself."

Jeremy nodded. "I'll remember that."

"Good. Two more things, Jeremy?"

"Sir?"

"Okay, three things. First, you're too good a boy to not find someone that deserves you. Patience, lad. Patience."

Jeremy knew he wasn't good at patience. But he was good at losing himself in a project. He'd merely need to find the right project and he'd be well distracted.

"Second, I'm not a sir."

Jeremy managed a weak smile. "Yes sir."

"Third," Jack's voice sounded ready to laugh for the first time in days, "aren't you supposed to be getting your ass out of here? You leave for school tomorrow, right?"

"But..." Jeremy waved a hand helplessly at the empty and crippled admin center.

Jack's hearty slap sent Jeremy stumbling forward. "Not your problem, young Master Jeremy, so don't make it your problem. I've been at this game long enough to know how it's played. I already put out a call and help is on its way. Now clear out your station and get to where you're supposed to be going."

Jeremy moved to his old station. After double checking that he *had* fully delinked from the C-5M Galaxy, he carefully closed and collapsed his simulation controller.

His father's story came to mind of the C-5 Galaxy that

had flown immediately prior to his own rescue flight; the one that had crashed into a rice paddy, killing so many.

Jeremy did a quick search to see what had caused it.

April 1975 and Saigon was falling, the North Vietnamese were everywhere, the locals were stealing any piece of the wrecked plane they could for use on their farms.

Yet an investigation team had gone in. They purchased key pieces of the wreckage from the locals. A dive team had found the rear door and the cockpit voice recorder in the ocean close offshore. They had even tracked down the maintenance teams in the midst of the evacuation and interviewed them to determine the cause.

Parts had been in such short supply that the rear ramp locks of the C-5 had been scavenged to fix other planes. In the final rush, one maintenance team had failed the aircraft for flight. Due to collapsing communication and not knowing about the first team's report, a second team inspected the plane and missed the locking mechanism's disrepair. With five out of seven locking mechanisms inoperative, the remaining two couldn't hold the massive ramp closed as the Galaxy had climbed to altitude. There been an explosive decompression, which had blown off the gate and damaged the tail and the hydraulic systems past recovery.

Those men, back then it had probably only been men, had risked their lives to solve a crash in a war zone to save lives in the future. And for Penelope, he'd taken over one of those same planes as if it was a toy.

He dumped his personal files into a secure cloud storage. Which only left...

The MIT course catalog.

It was open to mechanical engineering. Fourth down was aeronautical engineering.

He stared at it for a long time before he realized what he *had* to do. In recompense for what he'd almost done...

No. He *hadn't* done it. Not even when he could have let Penelope and the others off the hook, he'd finally done what was right.

But if he didn't want to be like her, who did he *want* to be like?

The men who had flown *into* a collapsing war zone to solve a plane crash so that more, like his father, wouldn't be killed in the future.

He closed the catalog, knowing what he had to do now. He'd never be the guy they sent into harm's way like Jack Donovan. But just as his father designed the Flight Simulator to help train safer piloting skills, he'd make sure the planes themselves were safer. He'd stay away from computers, which meant no Microsoft, and lose himself in investigating plane crashes. Solving those puzzles so that he could make sure that the next flight would make it through.

Jeremy patted his console and signed off.

He turned and made it half out of his chair before collapsing back into it. He landed so hard that he flopped the chair over backwards and banged his head on the floor.

Lyra had been looking over his shoulder without him noticing.

Jack's big laugh boomed out. Jack then stepped up and slipped a hand around Lyra's waist.

"I know exactly how you feel, young Master Jeremy. She

did the exact same thing to me when I met her. Exact same thing." Then he kissed her on the temple.

Jeremy struggled to his feet and decided that Jack was right about many things. He too would wait until someone simply knocked his feet out from under him.

ACKNOWLEDGMENTS

John E. Jack Donovan, while a member of the Army Security Agency (ASA), served two tours in Vietnam as a combat electronic warfare intelligence analyst. During the '68 Tet Offensive, his unit was pinned down and nearly overrun. He knew full well, because of his specialty in intel, that capture would mean torture and death. Despite this, when a buddy's wife was suffering from a medical emergency, he upped for a second tour and returned to Vietnam in his friend's place.

Twenty years later, he served once more in electronic intelligence along the North Korean borders and others during the height of the Cold War—this time from the relative safety of the air. Towards the end of his time spent in the intelligence field, he was indeed eased out of the service for asking too many questions about the intel he continued to uncover.

With a degree in hotel management, he met and eventually married his Lithuanian love, who he claims definitely keeps him on his toes. He really was the soldier primarily responsible for the amendment of Army Regulation 670-1 authorizing soldiers to wear a POW/MIA bracelet while in uniform. It is still his proudest achievement from those awful years. A day does not go by that he doesn't remember those who fell. Please feel free to join him in donating to his favorite charity, the USO. They directly help our servicemen and women in so many more ways than simple entertainment: https://www.uso.org/

ANDI DISCOVERS WHAT'S IN A NAME

Before she joined Miranda Chase's air-crash investigation team, **Captain Andi Wu** *wasn't born a Night Stalkers helicopter pilot. She was born to be a lawyer and spend her life in the family's highly prestigious San Francisco law firm.*

Little did she know that a single day would change the entire flight plan of her life.

1

San Francisco International Airport

"ANOTHER DAY, ANOTHER DIRTY LITTLE JOB." ANDREA HATED that she was quoting Mother. It was an inevitable Wu family disease as Ching Hui Wu completely lived up to her name's meaning, Capable Clever Business, and she had a maxim for every situation—especially Andrea's *dirty little job.*

"It's not enough that I'm four-oh at Stanford Law," she told her helicopter as she ran through the preflight check for her night job—executive air-taxi pilot flying all over the San Francisco Bay area.

You do know that a Wu need never work except in law?

"Yes, Mother. I know." Andrea tried to match Mother's tone of dripping sarcasm...but couldn't do so credibly to her own ear, even in private. She'd *never* make it as a trial lawyer for the family's firm of Wu and Wu. That meant she'd be spending the rest of her life lost in Mother's shadow drafting trusts and court filings for others. Could there possibly be a gloomier thought?

Which was ridiculous. The skies were clear, the summer fogs had finally rolled out to sea leaving San Francisco Bay, which surrounded the airport on most of three sides, to shine in the late afternoon light.

As a bonus, though she only had one flight tonight, it was perfectly timed so that she'd at least miss the traditional extended-family end-of-week dinner—at which her own deficiencies were always a main course. That was worth cheering about. As no other pilots or mechanics were in the hangar at the moment, Andrea gave a small *whoop* and felt better for it.

The Wu family law firm traced its roots straight back to the importation of workers for the building of the Transcontinental Railroad in the 1860s—which was total horseshit. They'd been the Chens when they'd reached San Francisco barely ahead of the Mao Communist Revolution of 1949. That they'd arrived with their fortune intact—long since converted into handy gold and jewelry by a savvy ancestor—had certainly helped matters.

By 1952, they'd purchased the prestigious firm of Wu and Wu LLP, changed the family name from Chen, and taken over. Wu and Wu's partners were forcibly retired as soon as the first new-Wu made it through law school and the bar exam. The new-Wus were just as adaptable to the times as the old-Chens.

The firm soon specialized in intellectual property law, another savvy move that had nicely anticipated the rise of Silicon Valley. The growth of the family fortune hadn't faltered for a moment. This was enforced by partnerships being restricted to family members. Only the most menial of associates weren't related.

This was such a well-known fact that Andrea had received five thinly disguised proposals during her first year at Stanford Law from men who aspired to marry in. This year there had already been three more and September wasn't over yet.

Going anywhere other than Wu and Wu for copyright or trademark law is worse than bad business, it's foolishness, Mother could deliver the line to a CEO without making it sound condescending. *We helped* write *the Copyright Act of 1976, after all.* That, at least, was technically true. Uncle Bob Wu had been a clerk in charge of photocopies for a minor US Senator who'd been on the drafting committee.

Andrea had always liked Uncle Bob, the black sheep; he was the last Wu to ever clerk for less than a federal judge. Not so *bright and shining* as his first name had foretold. He was also the only one who didn't look down on her night job of flying an executive air-taxi helo out of San Francisco International.

She completed the preflight checklist and turned to the engine prestart checklist. It went quickly as Bay Heli-air's newest helo was in perfect condition. During the day, it was the chief pilot's bird, but weeknights she'd pulled the lucky straw for reasons she didn't begin to understand and the luxury Bell 429WLG five-seater was all hers.

In Andrea's estimation, her dirty little job had two things going for it: she liked flying, and Mother hated it. *Wus were intended to ride in executive helicopters, not perform such a plebian chore as to actually fly them.* In fact, Mother hated it so much that she rarely mentioned the two possible benefits that Andrea had tried offering: chatting up wealthy passengers as potential future clients for Wu and Wu— which was never going to happen—and meeting a rich Chinese husband—which was even less likely.

A Wu never settles, Andrea. You will restrict your dalliances to proper American-born Chinese persons.

Andrea was not superstitious, but she counted Mother's chosen phrasing, *persons,* as a stroke of great luck. The reason that she had less-than-zero interest in finding a husband was a discussion she still hadn't had with her parents despite being twenty-three. It was a level of being such a complete chicken about familial confrontation that it had cost her three different girlfriends, and still she'd never dared mention her choice—even though it wasn't a choice at all.

She could hear Mother's response: *A Wu would never be so sick. Until you are cured, you will see—* And Mother would have some therapist, quack, psycho on tap because she was never caught without an answer. She was named Capable Clever Business after all.

It had been a mystery to Andrea that anyone in the family had a Western first name. At least not until Uncle Bob had explained that it had nothing to do with anyone finally accepting their new country, and everything to do with making Wu and Wu more approachable for Californian business magnates. Grandmother still didn't understand how ridiculous Bob Wu was as a corporate lawyer's name.

With the helo's twin engines started and up to operating temperature, she contacted SFO ground control and received permission to air taxi to the Signature Executive Terminal. She still wasn't quite used to the new bird. The

Bell 429WLG GlobalRanger had added several enhancements over the 429, including the switch from skids to wheeled landing gear—hence the WLG. But having gotten clearance for the fun of an air-taxi rather than a slow and bumpy ground-taxi to the client's pickup point, she took the opportunity to fly at a one-meter hover. She gently touched down at the terminal building on the northeast corner of the airport across the runway from San Francisco International's main terminal.

Bay Heli-Air insisted on pilots always being five minutes early for any client pickup. She checked her clock—nailed it with five seconds to spare. She considered holding the hover for five extra seconds, but that felt like cheating. BHA's chief pilot, a former Marine Corps flier, was compulsive about schedules. His rules were so strict that the other pilots jokingly called it Hell-Air. Personally, she'd taken his rules as a personal challenge to outperform every one of his pilot mandates. She wasn't competitive, it was too trite a word to describe a Wu, even a *disappointment* like herself.

It was a lovely late-September evening, with only wisps of fog crawling by, so she settled to line up with the driveway gap between the terminal and the service hangar. The position made her most visible to anyone arriving on the shuttle from the main terminal, and it gave her a lovely view of San Francisco Bay out toward Oakland.

There she settled, cycled the engines down, and, ignoring the view, dutifully tugged out her thirteen-hundred-page tome of Ayres and Klass *Studies in Contract Law*. If she wanted to keep ahead at Stanford Law, every five minutes of extra study mattered.

Thirty minutes later she'd fended off two Signature Air

ground controllers who didn't want her cluttering up their small parking apron, and she had three pages of notes on breach-of-contract clauses. Andrea had checked the client's flight status and Megan Connelly's plane had landed on time but—

"I'm so sorry that I'm late," a woman in her thirties came trotting up to the door Andrea had kept propped open to the cool air.

"Not a problem, ma'am. Beautiful spot to sit." She nodded toward the late afternoon light splashing across the bay. While the woman looked toward the vista, Andrea carted her bags over to tuck them in the aft cargo compartment under the tail. Even though it was a solo flight, there was no reason to clutter the cabin.

Waiting was fine with Andrea, she was on the clock, so she was paid sitting or flying.

Tonight's client didn't look like the typical executive who used a four-thousand-dollar-an-hour helicopter service. Andrea was used to men in either Hugo Boss suits or dressed down in stone-washed jeans that cost as much as a pair of Mother's Jimmy Choos. They always had a telltale giveaway, other than looking too slick, of either the Montblanc leather briefcase for the lawyers or the Hermes iPad portfolio for the Silicon Valley techno geeks.

Their female counterparts were rare and they were habitually dressed better than the men. When traveling as a couple, the women always outshone them completely. And while some of them were very nice to look at, not one drew Andrea. The whole buffed-and-polished-like-a-prize vibe actually creeped her out. Give her a quietly brilliant woman sharing a burger and pint any day.

Ms. Connelly was five-foot-four, just two inches taller than Andrea. Lightly built, on her it looked slender rather than childlike as Andrea did. She wore her hair in a thick riffle of cedar-brown hair down past her shoulders. Her clothes were, Andrea had to blink, Wrangler jeans and she had a Carhartt jacket draped over one arm. The kind of clothes worn by people who worked outdoors in all weather. She had neither briefcase nor portfolio, just an REI knapsack the size of a largish purse.

"The local FAA office had a few questions for me," Megan explained as an apology.

Andrea flinched. Like a cop suddenly beside her car or Mother's knock on her bedroom door even when she wasn't doing anything, FAA inspectors could portend neutral or horrid circumstances to a pilot. They must be allergic to *good* news as they never delivered any.

A quick mental review convinced her that all of her paperwork was in order and she hadn't done anything questionable during any recent flight. No one else in sight except for the Signature Air guy guiding a sleek Gulfstream G650 bizjet into position.

The woman had to be very highly placed in the FAA to warrant an executive helicopter flight. *My tax dollars at work,* Mother remarked dryly in Andrea's thoughts.

She covered her nerves by asking, "Are you ready, ma'am?"

"I'm not a ma'am. I'm a Megan," and she held out her hand. Another thing that the male executives didn't do. They were often surprised at her diminutive stature—five-two didn't exactly make her loom beside her helo. Some had even requested to see her license to make sure she was old enough to fly. But once convinced she wasn't twelve, they ignored her existence as anything more than an extension of her helicopter.

"Andrea Wu."

Megan laughed. "Sorry, not quite a name I was expecting. That will teach me."

"You're saying I don't look like an Andrea?" she offered a smile.

"Maybe a Sue. Or a Bob," Megan teased. Another tone of voice Andrea rarely achieved.

"Bob's my uncle. Seriously, Uncle Bob Wu."

"Okay, I give up." Megan threw up her hands in resignation and laughed again. No one in the Wu family was much given to laughter. "Lead on, Andrea."

Andrea slid back the side door to the four deep armchairs, mini-fridge, and entertainment center. But Megan's glance drifted toward the copilot's seat. "It's fine to sit up front if you'd prefer."

Megan nodded and circled around.

Andrea shifted *Studies in Contract Law* from the passenger seat to the rear, then completed a last walkaround, mostly to ensure that her passenger had latched her door properly. Megan had, and also properly belted herself in and was wearing the spare headset.

Andrea had never heard of surprise FAA inspections. What kind of trouble was she in?

2

AFTER HUSTLING, WITHOUT *LOOKING* LIKE SHE WAS HUSTLING, Andrea took them aloft and turned south-southwest headed for the hills above Santa Cruz. The Pacific Ocean became a sweeping vista of gold as the sun settled below the horizon of the offshore fog banks.

It was such a lovely evening that she dropped flight-following advisories, where local air traffic control tracked her every move. Instead, she climbed to three thousand feet and stayed west of the Santa Cruz Mountains which climbed up past four thousand, practically scraping against the six thousand-foot bottom of SFO controlled airspace. Tonight was so clear that all she needed was her GPS and her traffic radar for spotting other aircraft.

"That's so much better," Megan offered once Andrea was done with the radio work and in the clear. She scrubbed at her face with both hands. If she wore makeup, it didn't show before or after that.

"Hard trip?" Andrea wasn't well prepared to have a chatty

passenger; in two years it had happened a grand total of never.

"Ten regional offices in the last ten weeks. But I'm finally done. Someone must have decided that I deserved a helo flight home and I'm not complaining."

She hit all ten regional FAA offices? There were centers from Hawaii to New England, and Alaska to the southeastern US. But it didn't sound as if Andrea herself was under any investigation. Despite assuring herself that no one so high up in the FAA could care about a mere pilot, Andrea could feel herself tightening up anyway.

"Are you okay?" Megan Connelly was also too astute an observer.

Andrea forced herself to relax by brute force—which failed miserably. "Other than each of my flight tests, it's the first time I've had an FAA official aboard."

"Ooo! Am I scary? I always wanted to be scary, but my kids say that I'm a complete failure in that department."

"Yes!" Andrea blurted it out. "Well, scarier than Mister Corporate Executive Number Eighty-four who is convinced of his own self worth beyond all—" She clamped her mouth shut. Another Hell-Air policy was to never trash talk any client, ever. That was *not* one of Mother's policies. Raking clients' reputations over a dish of spicy Ma Po Tofu or Dan Dan Pork Noodles at the dinner table was a favorite family pastime.

"Excellent. Will it ruin it for you if I tell you that I'm a curriculum writer for the FAA? I design and write the coursework for inspectors and air traffic controllers."

Andrea managed to unearth a small laugh as the gold sunset shifted into pinks. She'd edged westward to follow the coast south because it was so pretty after the long summer fogs.

"Or I was..." Megan's tone was suddenly wistful over the headset.

"Was?"

"Today was my last day. I'm now officially retired except for occasional consulting."

Andrea twisted to look at her. Wus didn't retire. At eighty-three, Great-grandmother still ran Wu and Wu with the same iron fist that had taken it over when she was twenty-one. She was the only Wu who didn't have a law degree and didn't practice law, instead managing all aspects of the firm. The family always said that she didn't need a degree because she was a law unto herself. No one *ever* said it jokingly.

"I know. It feels very strange. I've been doing it for twenty years and suddenly I'm done." Megan gave an eloquent shrug.

Andrea followed the curve of the coastline out to Pescadero Point. Twenty years from now she herself would be still just another Wu lawyer. She shuddered, but managed not to let it be reflected in the controls. *Sixty* years from now would she be the iron fist of Wu and Wu, feared by all? Even Mother was cowed when Great-grandmother slammed the foot of her cane on the floor like a judge's gavel.

"What will you do now?"

Megan smiled brightly and half turned in her seat to face Andrea. "Oh, we've always had this dream, my husband and my three kids. I've got two boys and a girl. She's my youngest and is one of those twelve-on-the-verge-of-twenty types and loves finding trouble. My oldest is JROTC and about to get his driving license which is even scarier. We sold our place in Florida, dumping jobs and everything. We just bought a horse ranch in the hills above Santa Cruz. It's been our dream since forever and now it's coming true. We're going to specialize in rehab for horses, as well as for disabled youth. My middle boy is on the autism spectrum and horses have been a great therapy treatment. Eventually I want to expand that into a para-equestrian training center."

"Para...equestrian?"

"Horsemanship for events like the Special Olympics. Horses are not smart except emotionally, but they're brilliant that way. That can work great with building confidence among these disabled kids. Bringing the two together should be amazing!" Megan's hands, which had been laying quietly in her lap while discussing the FAA, were now drawing pictures across the darkening sky as she effused with a staggering degree of excitement.

Andrea tightened her grip slightly on the joystick above her lap, not in panic this time but just in case Megan slapped hers. The only time she ever felt that way herself...was definitely not while studying torts and contracts.

Megan kept talking happily about her plans for the last few minutes of the flight. An hour by road, except on a Friday evening like tonight when it would be two or three, had lasted but a quick twenty minutes by air. Over Monterey Bay, where a few late evening surfers from UC Santa Cruz were still testing the waves in the last of the twilight, she turned southeast and began her descent as the hills began their ascent.

Megan leaned forward to watch as the helo slowed.

"Settle in the big corral behind the house. I don't think our horses are much used to helicopters."

Andrea flicked on the landing lights and circled once to inspect the area. Cleared out of the oak and Douglas fir woods there was a lodge, a barn, a caretaker's house, and several corrals of varying sizes. A smaller one was filled with obstacles for jumping, but a larger one was empty of horses and offered her plenty of room to put down forty-three feet of helicopter safely.

During the final descent, two large dogs raced toward the helo as if they could scare her back into the sky. The downdraft of the rotors pushed them back hard enough that they weren't going to get under her wheels.

Megan was laughing by the time Andrea had settled in the ankle-high grass.

"Those silly pups. Hamlin is the Malinois and Luna is some sort of a black golden retriever something. Don't worry, they're all bark and no bite."

"I think my helicopter can take it," Andrea spun the engine throttle down to idle and doused the blinding landing light. She did keep an eye on the dogs as she stepped out to retrieve Megan's luggage.

There wasn't any need. The instant Megan was on the grass and called out a greeting, the dogs stormed her with happy yips. The three of them tumbled together onto the thick pasture grass.

Any Wu dog was mandated to be no larger than a Shih Tzu and no less hairy (or ridiculous) than a Pekingese—and, of course, Chinese in origin and of show quality. Wu dogs *always* placed high in regional competitions.

Uncle Bob owned a rather rambunctious standard

poodle that couldn't win a show that included any other poodle but was a complete sweetheart. *Black dog for the black sheep,* Mother dripped disdain at every chance. No wonder Uncle Bob rarely came to dinners anymore. If only she could figure out how to do that herself.

"Sorry," Megan didn't sound the least bit apologetic as she regained her feet, keeping low until she stood well clear of the nine-foot-high rotor blades and stopped beside Andrea.

"They seem happy to see you."

"The feeling is mutual. Usually I work from home, but I think the FAA wanted to leach every last bit out of me while they still could." Megan shrugged as if she'd enjoyed it.

Mother would leach a Wu lawyer to skin and bones if it served to— Andrea shrugged off the thought. She felt more...hopeful, just for being around Megan.

"How can I be like you?" The words slipped out.

For once, Megan didn't laugh. The dogs were still bounding around her and the rotor blades were swinging lazily across the night sky. Only the dim cockpit lights and the moon lit the pasture. A single porch light shone on the front of the house.

Andrea could see Megan's family coming down the steps as well.

Megan snapped her fingers and aimed a finger at the ground. The two dogs instantly lay down on the grass but kept their eyes on their mistress.

Megan continued to watch her and it was only family training for parties that saved Andrea from shuffling her feet.

"What are you doing tomorrow?"

Nine to noon, Legal Ethics study group. Noon to three, self-study of Global Litigation. Three— "I don't have any plans."

"Excellent. Come down. We'll go riding."

"On horses?" Horseback riding was *not* a Wu family activity.

Megan looked torn between a laugh and shock. "Unless you'd rather try riding Hamlin here?" She pointed down at the waiting Malinois.

"Your family..."

"They already have other plans. Come, I'll show you how to ride."

Missing the Legal Ethics study group for any reason short of being in an actual coma was grounds for possible expulsion. Andrea looked at the wide pasture and the tall trees etched black against the stars. She listened to the soft whirr of the idling engines and the steady beat of the rotor blades. Then she turned and looked north toward Stanford and the Wu mansion high on Presidio Heights.

"Thanks, I'll be here."

They shook on it, then Megan turned and was enveloped by her family.

Andrea slipped back into the pilot's seat and eased aloft as quietly as she could.

3

IT WAS AN HOUR'S DRIVE FROM HER APARTMENT NEAR
Stanford to Megan's ranch. Andrea sat for twenty minutes at
the foot of the driveway. If she turned around and rushed
back, she'd be only half an hour late for study group, but
that could be blamed on oversleeping due to a late flight.
Though lying to a group studying legal ethics...

She resisted thumping her head against the steering
wheel—an action Mother drove her to so often.

The sole ethical course of action remaining was to keep
her commitment to visit Megan Connelly and face the
fallout of the study group later. *I had an appointment with the
FAA I couldn't change.* No, still past the gray line that bothered
so few of her fellow students.

One other factor tipped her decision. Mother always said
how important names were. Andrea had looked it up last
night; Megan Connelly translated into Gaelic as Pearl Fierce-
as-a-hound.

Andrea knew that was something completing lacking in

her personality, but it had looked so wonderful last night as Megan had played with her dogs and been greeted by her family.

She put the car in Drive and headed uphill along the tree-lined driveway.

Through the trees to the left of the driveway, she caught glimpses of an estate worthy of the Wu family, including a vast swimming pool, outdoor verandah, and a sprawling multistory mansion that looked vaguely Victorian. To the right stood the better-screened back of an old clapboard house that desperately needed either paint or a bulldozer.

But the drive didn't branch toward either house which must have entrances of their own. The end of the tree-lined driveway slipped out into the open and landed her in front of a cozy timber lodge to the right, a barn and covered corral to the left, and straight ahead several arenas and the big corral she'd landed in. The drive ended at the modest house that Megan's family had emerged from last night.

"A Mini-Cooper. Eminently practical," Megan greeted her from where she sat on the porch steps with her two dogs lying on the porch behind her. She wore jeans, boots, and a t-shirt that said *My other car is a horse.*

"A mini car for a mini person," Andrea offered her standard response.

Megan laughed, much more honestly than most did.

"Actually Mother is horrified that it isn't an Audi or a Mercedes."

"She cares?" Megan sent her a questioning look as she raised a thermos over a second mug.

"You have no idea. 'We of the Wu family must always

represent our best selves to our clientele.' It never ends."
Andrea sat on the steps and took the proffered cup.

"Hot chocolate, dark. I hope you don't mind."

Andrea hadn't been allowed hot chocolate since she was
twelve...and missed it. "Sounds great!"

Megan didn't say anything, so Andrea sat in silence
unsure what to do next as she sipped the lush cocoa. She
should never have revealed that she came from money; it
made people act so strangely. At school, it was almost
mandatory—family millions was the minimum entry level
for being invited into certain key cliques that, frankly, she
never wanted to be a member of in the first place.

But Megan didn't appear to be judging anything, but
instead seemed content to sit and watch the day.

"Where's your family?"

"They all went into town for the day, but it was my first
day home in so long, that I wanted to sit and listen to the
quiet."

"If I'm in the way..." Andrea started to rise, but Megan
waved her back to her step.

"You're my excuse to play with the horses, not that I need
one."

It was a few hours past sunrise. The last crispness of the
September morning was giving away to the sun reaching
over the tall trees. The silence was so deep that it made her
ears ring. A Steller's jay clung to a rail for a moment, chirped
a question, and honed its beak quickly on either side of the
rail before flitting away. Other birds flitted about the yard. In
the corral by the barn, five horses stood lazily. Two tugged at
a pile of hay and she could actually hear the swishing of
their tails as they slapped to either side.

"I don't think I've ever been somewhere this quiet."

"Quiet but full," Megan sighed happily, then set her mug by the thermos. "Ready?"

"For what? No, never mind. I'm here, so I guess I'm ready."

"Good," Megan gave her a hand up. "Hmmm. Hang on." She ducked through the front door and came back with a pair of boots. "I'm sorry for this next line, but I think my twelve-year-old daughter's boots should fit you. You can't wear sneakers around a horse in case they accidentally step on you."

"Step on me?" Andrea looked at her feet and could feel their pain already.

"Not a big deal usually, but their metal horseshoes can easily tear through a sneaker which is never good."

Andrea dutifully took off her running shoes, too late for running away now, and pulled on Megan's young daughter's boots. They fit perfectly.

4

"YOU'VE REALLY NEVER BEEN AROUND HORSES?"

"I've seen the mounted police in Golden Gate Park but that's about it."

Megan just shook her head as she led them from the porch over toward the corral of lazing horses. "I can't remember a time when I didn't know how to ride. I apparently started riding in Mom's sling when I was about eight weeks old."

"I sometimes think I was raised on the witness stand." Her nanny had probably decorated her crib with successful Wu and Wu court rulings.

"No one here but us horses." As Megan approached the split-rail fence, the horses shook off the somnambulance and bobbed their way over.

The police horses had always looked big, but she'd never had reason to be close to one. Andrea had never connected that the horses were *so* much bigger than she was. Their heads were as big as her torso.

"Here," Megan handed her a cube of sugar fit for an afternoon tea. "Put it in the open flat of your palm, tuck your thumb in tight to the side, and curve your fingers back. Then just hold it out."

"But it's so small. Shouldn't it be horse-sized?"

"They go nuts for sugar cubes. About the closest there is to a horse drug. Better than apples."

"But—"

"Trust me."

Andrea did as she was told. A horse the dusty-yellow color of aged parchment, with legs and a muzzle the color of Indian ink, stretched its neck much farther over the rail than Andrea had thought possible. Before she could react, the horse raised a lip revealing massive teeth, then swept up the sugar so gently that she could barely feel the motion.

The horse gave a happy crunch or two, then stretched out again, and blew a tornado of air at her out of its nostrils. She closed her eyes against the dry hay smell as her hair flapped in the brief wind.

"There. Now Raya, short for Ray-a-Sunshine, will remember you as the one with the sugar cubes. Rub her nose," Megan demonstrated on a big brown that had come up alongside begging for his own sugar cube. Andi wasn't sure what she expected, but it wasn't what she touched between the palm-sized nostrils.

"It's so soft. Is it all—" she rubbed her hand higher along the horse's nose. "Nope, much coarser."

"Try this." Megan made her fingers into a claw shape and scrubbed vigorously at her horse's broad cheek.

When she did, the horse leaned into it and its huge liquid eyes rolled partly shut. The fur was coarse but she could feel the powerful jaw muscles under the thick hide. Raya let out a very horsey sigh of contentment.

"You don't show any fear." Megan was watching closely.

"Should I be?"

"No. But it's very unusual in a first timer. Still, I'm not going to be putting you up on Pioneer Bill—he's a handful even after a sugar-cube bribe. He's PB for short, but you've got to watch your peanut butter sandwiches around him; he really loves PB&J."

Andrea let herself get lost in the processes that followed. Scrubbing over Raya's hide with a circular brush called a curry comb to release all of the dirt and dead skin. She even managed to clean the hooves, though she was a long way from having a knack for it. The pick looked rather fiercesome to be digging into a horse foot but Raya didn't seem to mind.

And when she was all combed and perfect, including her mane and tail, Raya knelt down and rolled over into the dirt.

"Raya!"

Megan laughed. "She always does that. Some horses only take a rare dust bath when the ticks and such are really bothering them, but Raya must be part hippopotamus, she loves a good dirt bath."

"Well, you're not going to get all brushed out again, you hear?"

The horse looked at her.

"Is that chagrin?"

"It depends," Megan looked over her shoulder and down at the horse.

"On what?"

Raya clambered back to her feet, gave herself a great

shake that filled the air with dust and flopped her ears back and forth as if they were disconnected. Then she laughed. It was the only word Andrea had for the sound.

"It depends on that," Megan said. "Yes, horses can laugh."

"Great, a giant sarcastic horse. Exactly what I need," though Andrea dusted off the soft tip of Raya's nose to show there were no hard feelings.

"She's not a giant; she's only sixteen hands."

"Hands?"

"Hands. Four inches, from side-to-side of your hands across your knuckles."

"More like twenty-one Andrea hands," she held up her hand to demonstrate.

"Doesn't mean you can't do great things with them."

"At twenty-one Andrea hands it certainly means that I can't see over Raya's back."

"Well, let's fix that."

5
<hr/>

MEGAN HAD CERTAINLY FIXED THAT.

"I can see the whole world from up here." Perched up in Raya's saddle, she did feel a very long way from the ground, far higher than when flying safe in her helo. "As long as I don't fall off and kill myself. Though that would get me out of Sunday dinner which could be a fair trade."

Megan stopped fooling with the stirrups. "Are they that bad?"

"Last night, Friday, was the weekly all-family dinner but Sundays are immediate family only. Mother has fewer targets on Sunday including yours truly. Of course, Grandmother unloads her fair share on Mother's head, which is always fun to watch."

"You sound close, but..."

"But not," Andrea agreed so emphatically that Raya twitched her head around to stare at her sitting perched up in the saddle.

Andrea leaned forward to pat her reassuringly on the

neck, but felt as if she was going to pitch off, either gutting herself on the Western pommel at the front of the saddle, or ending up in the dust at a laughing horse's feet. She managed a small pat before recovering to upright.

"Father states that being a member of the Wu family should be a televised blood sport. Only the wiliest survive."

"Are you wily?" Megan snapped a stout line to the side of Raya's bridle.

Andrea sighed. "Not at all. It is seen as a criminal lack among the Wu."

"You make it sound like a cult, or perhaps a genetic experiment."

Andrea's gut wound into a knot. It was *exactly* like that. She—

Her world abruptly shifted!

The saddle was no longer a high, fixed seat, but tilted in several directions simultaneously. Coaxed by the halter rope, Raya stepped forward but there was a side shift as well.

Andrea grabbed for the pommel.

"No, don't touch that. Keep your weight in your butt and thighs. Think of yourself melting against the saddle."

She froze her hands inches from the pommel with all of the restraint learned as a pilot. Small changes, small corrections.

Raya took another step.

And the world shifted the other way. Megan led her around the corral at a slow walk.

"Feel the flexibility in your hips."

"In a helicopter, it's in your wrists and ankles." And it had long since become so natural that she was wholly unconscious of it. Flying was also about not freezing. There was no way to keep a truly soft wrist if her shoulders were clenched. A loose ankle sensitive to the slightest pressure change on the rudders couldn't be done with locked hips.

She let herself go with Raya's flow, taking note of Megan's tips and suggestions. Weight in the butt and thighs, not the stirrups. Not heel down but rather relaxed ankle. By the third lap around the corral, she became aware of the gentle bobbing of Raya's head with each step and the flutter of her mane in the light air from the motion. This time when she reached down to pat Raya's neck, her center of gravity didn't tumble from the sky, but remained anchored in the seat of the shifting saddle.

After two more laps at a faster walk, Megan stopped and looked up at her.

"What?"

"How did you do that so fast? I ask out of professional interest. I've trained a lot of riders, and few adapt so quickly."

Andrea leaned forward and scrubbed her fingers against Raya's neck; she was answered by a bridle-gangling head shake and ear flap.

"I'm a helo pilot. Raya is just like a very slow helicopter bobbling through the complex air currents around San Francisco Bay."

"Well, that's a new one on me. You must be a natural in the air."

Andrea opened her mouth, then closed it again. She remembered her latest flight with the chief pilot, who made a point of going aloft with every pilot at least once a quarter.

For her entire check ride in BHA's newest helicopter, Marine Corps Major Wolfson hadn't said a word about the flight except for calling out the next maneuver. She'd read the Bell 429WLG's manual, of course, and memorized all of the emergency checklists before the flight. He rode his hands on the second set of controls the entire time. As she practiced climbs, stalls, turns around a point, hovers, and a score of other exercises, she'd felt the nuances of his control through the link.

By the end of the two-hour flight, she'd been both wrung out and completely hyper. It had been the first time she'd appreciated the true subtleties of a master pilot. She was finally good enough that she understood what he did and why. The last fifteen maneuvers had been repeating the ones she'd started with. His hands were on the controls, she could see them. But she'd adapted and they were in such perfect sync that she couldn't feel them.

Throughout the flight, he'd also quizzed her about the procedures and the aircraft, even during the trickiest of maneuvers. *A good pilot must be able to do five things at once—a great one at least ten.* He hadn't said a single word about her flying, simply nodding to her after the landing. The Bell 429WLG had been the assigned bird on her nightly flight sheet ever since.

"I'm...pretty good. I guess."

"Pretty good. *She guesses.*" Megan's laugh was lurking somewhere close to the surface. "Okay, let's test that theory."

6

MEGAN HAD KEPT THE LEAD ON RAYA'S BRIDLE, BUT IT WAS now trailing loosely from Megan's own horse, Pioneer Bill.

"We're not going to run, are we?"

"On a horse it's called trot, canter, or gallop in order of increasing speed. And no, I'm not that cruel to a new rider. My ranch is intended to instill confidence, not destroy it."

"You'd never survive at Wu and Wu," Andrea muttered to herself.

"Wu and Wu? The law firm?" Megan asked in a tone of distinct surprise.

Okay, she'd *meant* to mutter to herself, yet another failed skill. She nodded.

"I thought they were all lawyers. You fly helicopters."

"I enjoy it. It's the only part of my life that's for me. The rest is Stanford Law. Did you like the FAA?" Hopefully that would distract Megan. She was lovely; slender without looking like an Andrea-sized adolescent. She had a family that had looked really close last night, and she was so... excited about her life. How would it feel to be like that?

"I loved the FAA." Megan stepped into her saddle with such practiced ease, like an old Western movie cowboy...cowgirl.

Not the answer Andrea had been expecting. It was a job, a chore. She should be happy to escape it.

"Creating curricula is actually a very complex and fascinating task. Keeping everyone engaged while discussing safety that could save lives is no easy feat. Making sure that not just best practices, but best results are enhanced as much as possible. I like keeping current with the latest news and techniques, and fussing all of those details into place, it makes me happy. Especially knowing that it could save lives. A lot of information flows in from the NTSB about air-crash investigations that I had to incorporate as well. To save even more lives. But this?"

She waved a hand out and upward to encompass the horses, the trees, and the blue sky above the corral.

"This was always the dream. Is Wu and Wu your dream?"

Andrea could only snort with a half-laughter/half-choking cough to relieve the gut-wrenching pain. It was a good thing that she'd been too nervous to eat more than a yogurt cup this morning.

"I'll take that as a no." Megan then pointed beyond the corral. "Let's go for a trail *walk*. Nothing faster. No... running." She offered a smile.

Her voice shifted to almost a classroom tone and Andrea could feel herself being soothed.

"Work on staying relaxed. Like a pilot, keep a firm but

calm hand on the reins—horses read emotions down the reins. Without firm control, Raya will think she can stop to graze on grass or a bush and when she puts her head down, too tight a grip on the reins can drag you right out of the saddle. I have the rope, so it will be okay to let go, but it's better if you control her in the first place." Then leaning down with the ease of long practice, Megan unlatched the corral gate, walked them through, and relatched it without dismounting.

She was as smooth and practiced on horses as Andrea was in the air. And she was parceling out technique at just the rate Megan judged Andrea herself could consume it. The two dogs, who had lain by the corral watching them through the morning, now bounded about, ready for action. Their horses appeared used to them.

Andrea had always thought of helos as living things: each definitely had its own personality. Raya was that times ten. She had odd movements that were slowly becoming familiar. And she certainly had a mind of her own. She tore a cluster of leaves off a bush and munched away on them placidly as she continued walking. An orange-and-black monarch butterfly little bigger then Raya's long eyelashes was watched carefully in case it attacked, but the squirrel shooting across the trail was beneath notice.

They rapidly moved from corral to pasture to trees and finally to shaded forest. The dogs raced into the underbrush, reappearing unexpectedly far down the trail. The world seemed thick and cool around her despite the warm September day.

Megan rode quietly in the lead, giving Andrea time to get

used to Raya's shifts as she walked along the roughness of the trail. She leaned out to look down at the meter-wide brook that Raya splashed through without so much as a glance. Did it feel cool on her hooves? Could her hooves even feel?

"Lean forward a little as she climbs the bank," Megan's voice was no louder than the birdsong which had become thicker along with the trees. The soft thudding beat of Raya's hooves was the only other sound.

Until a squirrel raced out on a branch over the trail, looked down and yelled at the horses for being so rude as to intrude in her part of the forest.

In answer Raya raised her head in alarm, then offered a loud snort of disgust that spooked the squirrel back to the tree.

"Good girl." Andrea leaned forward to pat Raya's neck. "You show that squirrel who's boss."

Megan turned from her lead position, apparently trusting her horse to continue unattended. "She used to be very spooky about squirrels. It took a lot of training for her to break that fear response."

"To break the fear response..." Why did she have an image of Great-grandmother thumping her cane on the floor? Or the light in Mother's eye when she'd identified Andrea as her next target?

Megan turned back to the trail, chatting happily about how she'd helped Raya through the challenges, building her confidence.

But Andrea couldn't get those two images out of her mind.

"I finally taught her to be a horse and that squirrels were far beneath her notice."

She looked back along the trail but the branch was already out of sight. What was she supposed to do if she was the squirrel?

7

"ARE YOU READY?"

Andrea looked around, but couldn't see any cause for alarm. The sun had stayed steadily off her right shoulder, so they couldn't be coming back to the farm. That only left her with one possibility.

"You said no running."

"I did," Megan's smile *looked* trustworthy.

Judgement of character *was* one of her strengths, it just wasn't always conscious. But it had led her back to Megan instead of to Legal Ethics—the study group was probably voting her out right about now. Juried, judged, and executed *in absentia.*

She'd certainly voted to do the same to a male student who was consistently late. They'd simply moved the meeting location without notifying him, which had made the process painless, for them anyway.

"Then I guess I'm ready."

Megan turned silently back in her saddle as they turned

onto a side trail, and splashed through a deep brook that came to Raya's knees. In the middle, they turned upstream, splashing along for a hundred meters.

"Locals' secret," Megan whispered as they turned upslope out of the stream.

Andrea was pleased that she'd survived the lumpy passage of the stream and even remembered to ease her weight forward for the climb up the bank. She was less sure about coming back down the slope later but for once she wasn't going to worry about the future.

At the crest of the rise, they broke through in a clearing awash with low brush. About the clearing were red-brown trunks so massive, with such deeply crenulated bark that there was no mistaking what they were.

"A redwood grove," her whisper rang loud in the clearing that was silent except for the bit of brush Raya had torn up and was now chewing. She tipped her head back, and back, and... "There's no end to them."

"Nope," Megan agreed cheerfully. "They go straight to the sky. There are only fourteen full-grown trees in this group, but the smallest was measured at over two hundred and fifty feet. The monster is taller than a football field and has almost a quarter of a million board feet of lumber in her."

Though they were well-spaced, they were so massive that she could only count seven of them. "The Seven Dwarves."

"How did you know?"

"Know what?"

Megan waved at the trees. "That's the nickname of this grove, because you can only see the seven. The others are back through that way, farther up a section of the stream you aren't skilled enough yet to ride. We could walk it if you don't mind getting soaking wet."

"These are quite enough." The sunlight sliced between the trees like searchlight beams illuminating the shadowed grove in brilliant spangles.

"You've never seen a redwood?"

"The obligatory school trip across the Golden Gate to Muir Woods but, uh, there was this girl. I didn't pay much attention to the trees."

Again Megan laughed easily. "What happened to her?"

Andrea was unsure. She had thought they were getting serious but she'd been just trying on Andrea as an experiment. She'd ultimately gone to the prom with the men's soccer goalie and Andrea hadn't gone at all. "We lost touch."

"Too bad." Megan didn't question Andrea's preferences at all.

Mother had made her biases all too clear in the past about a neighbor's gay son that she'd hoped to pair Andrea with. *Money must marry money, you know. If you were woman enough, you could make him forget all that nonsense.* Maybe someday she'd be somewhere that money didn't matter.

And maybe someday she'd sprout wings and fly to the top of a redwood tree.

Of course, she did fly a helicopter.

8

THEY STOOD AT THE PORCH STEPS.

Raya once again freshly brushed and snoozing in the barn's shade where it overshadowed the corral.

Andrea once more wore her sneakers, though she had the distinct impression that they were the only part of her that didn't smell strongly of horse and leather.

"I—" Andrea laughed at herself. "How am I supposed to put into words how much I appreciated today?"

"Try saying thank you."

Megan laughed as she did exactly that.

"Would it be okay if I said something? Friend-to-friend?"

Andrea nodded.

"As we were riding, I was watching you. Your lack of fear, quick adaptability, and self-control are amazing. I realized as I thought back to your piloting of last night's flight, precisely where that skill comes from. That's so very rare. You should embrace that. And in the grove... I don't take a lot of people there. Are you aware of how much you were smiling? What were you thinking about?"

"Flying." It spilled out so abruptly that Andrea had to laugh at herself. "I pictured that I could hop onto one of those perfect sunbeams then fly my helicopter right past those treetops and into the sky."

"Not contracts or torts or trademarks?"

Andrea shuddered enough to elicit one of Megan's great laughs. "Thought never entered my mind. Which is a surprise of its own."

"Everything happens for a reason," Megan didn't explain her comment. "My advice?"

Andrea kept her mouth shut.

Megan made the exact gesture she had this morning and encompassed the horses, the trees, and the sky above the corral.

9

As Andrea drove back toward San Francisco, she couldn't get past that final gesture that Megan Connelly had made so effortlessly.

Fly.

She glanced at Ayres and Klass *Studies in Contract Law* squatting on the passenger seat like an angry troll under a bridge...and looked away quickly.

Rather than driving up the coast, she'd taken the scenic and the slowest route along Highway 9 that climbed up and down over the redwood-studded hills all the way from Santa Cruz towards Cupertino. She'd flown over much of this territory, but never given much thought to what was on the ground.

Now she couldn't think of anything else. Not the horses and trees, not the brooks and sunbeams. What she couldn't get over was the view of the sky, revealed fresh around each corner and over each crest. It was like she was looking up at a different life.

Along the road ahead lay Stanford, a thousand family dinners, and a lifetime in law.

Up above...

She glanced at the contracts book again.

A contract. One for a new life.

That's what she needed. How could she fly like BHA's chief pilot? But he hadn't always been that, just as Megan Connelly hadn't been a horse instructor until just yesterday. Before joining Bay Heli-Air he'd been Marine Corps Major Wolfson.

Once she was in range of a cell tower, she pulled over and tugged out her smartphone. She managed to coax directions out of the new mapping software.

10

THE WOMAN WHO GREETED HER AS SHE STEPPED THROUGH THE door was dressed in camouflage, with tan boots. She introduced herself as Sergeant James.

"Excuse me, can you tell me who are the best helicopter pilots?"

"Depends on the service, ma'am."

"I mean across all the services." Her own wave, so like Megan's indicated the posters and colors about the room. Army green, Air Force blue, Navy blue. And images of men and women in uniform, tanks, jets, even aircraft carriers.

"Hey! Marine, Air Force. You guys got a minute?" Two men popped up from the cubicles that were arranged farther into the room. They came over and the four of them were standing together near the front door.

Andrea noted that there were two men and a woman in civilian clothes, talking with other military-clad men. A good day for recruiting.

"Best helo unit?" Sergeant James tossed it out like a challenge.

"US Air Force pararescue." The Air Force Staff Sergeant was also in camo.

"HMX-1. You probably know them as Marine One." The Marine Gunnery Sergeant wore blue slacks and a khaki button-down as if to say the Marines were a cut above. Instead of Army tan, his boots were polished black.

Andrea turned to the women and waited.

"The US Army 160th SOAR—Special Operations Aviation Regiment airborne. They're also called the Night Stalkers."

The other two men didn't look ready to argue the point which definitely meant something.

"And how does one sign up to fly with them?"

"Not possible. The way they work is that after five years with a beyond perfect Army flying record, a Night Stalkers recruiter might, *might*, invite that flier to apply. Then there's an eighty-percent-plus failure rate during testing. If they were to accept women which they don't."

Andrea had to think about that. She wasn't afraid of the challenges, a Wu knew how to excel: find the very best person, then do better, then find the best person after that and so on. It was how she maintained her four-oh average at the toughest law school in the country.

Five years to qualify. The cracks were already there, Chief Pilot Wolfson had talked about them. Someday soon, women would be flying forward combat.

"Let's talk," she addressed Sergeant James.

The two guys looked amused and turned for their desks.

"For...you?" The woman looked at her rather skeptically.

She stood five-eight, much taller than Megan's five-four. And rather than slim and almost elegant, she looked powerful. Andrea's neck would already be sore from looking up at her if she wasn't so used to it from her own five-two.

"Yes."

The two guys stopped to listen as the sergeant explained, "A helicopter pilot is a very restricted MOS—Military Occupational Specialty. It requires a certain skill set and—"

Andrea held out her commercial pilot's license and her logbook that she'd grabbed as she'd climbed out of the car.

"You have over two thousand hours." The sergeant couldn't keep the surprise out of her voice.

"I've flown air-taxi five nights a week for most of two years now with Bay Heli-Air. Before that—"

"You fly for Major 'Jazzman' Wolfson?" The Marine asked in surprise.

Andrea laughed, which was a surprise in itself and she liked the way it felt. "I'm having trouble with the Jazzman part, but the other two are correct."

"Shit! Uh... Sorry about the language, ma'am. But the man is a legend in the Corps."

Andrea felt as if she finally understood how a courtroom worked: challenge, evidence, argument. She'd never connected the flow during mock trials very well, but at the moment she knew exactly what to do.

She pulled out her phone, hit the speed dial for Wolfson, and set it on speaker.

"Wu." He answered the phone with his tone dead flat.

"Jazzman."

He scoffed. "You've been talking to people."

"Recruiters."

There was such a long silence that the four of them standing in the Armed Forces Career Center had time to all look at each other.

"Who?"

"Marines, Army, and Air Force are all with me at the moment. I didn't really think ahead about this, but it all made perfect sense once I did. I listened to every story you ever told. And the way you fly. Up there with you in the 429 was the best feeling of my life. I want to fly with people like that."

There was another long silence.

"Well, shit. I'm about to lose my best pilot."

Andrea bobbled the phone and almost lost it to the hard floor. "Best?"

The Marine looked as shocked as she felt.

"Grab a clue, Andrea. And don't you ever dare back off or I'll come boot your ass. Now, Air Force would drop you in a cargo bird. Marines won't let you near one of their precious gunships. The Army. Get in with the 101st, the Screaming Eagles. Five years from now, you give me a call, and I'll make damned sure someone finds you."

"The 160th?"

"The 160th."

"I won't need your help, but thank you."

"No, Wu. No, I expect you won't." And he hung up without another word.

The silence lasted long past her tucking her phone away.

The Marine finally broke it with a low whistle, "Jazzman Wolfson called her his best. Ain't that something."

Andrea decided that it definitely was, and all she had to do was keep living up to that. *That* she knew how to do. Just make sure that every single day she was better than the day before.

After a lengthy interview filled with questions about family and motivation, Sergeant James nodded her head. "I wouldn't have expected it, but I think you'll be a good fit. Not many walk in cold, especially with your kind of background. And even fewer of those would work out, but you feel right, Ms. Wu. The military is a very highly regimented world that is not a good match for everyone."

"I had the best of training." The Wu family was *completely* about respecting hierarchy and finding a way to function within its tight bounds. And since Andi had been flying by gut-feel alone since she'd left Megan's ranch, she figured that the sergeant's gut-feel would be good enough.

Sergeant James pulled up a form on her screen. "Here's the contract we're going to fill in together, print out, and then you'll want to think about it. You can sign it here, but once you do, it's official. You can also wait until the next swearing-in ceremony occurs and sign it then. There is no second thoughts or buyer's remorse clause. It's—"

"I'm second-year Stanford Law, Sergeant. You don't need to explain contract law to me."

"Well, if you're that hot to trot, the next swearing-in ceremony is Monday. Two days from now. You'd head straight to Basic Training on Tuesday. Or you can do a DEP, a Delayed Entry/Enlistment Program, that lets you wait up to a year before reporting."

Andrea thought about Stanford Law—and didn't give a damn. Her apartment and all of those thousands of dollars of course books could burn right along with *Studies in Contract Law* that she'd use to start the pyre.

Mother? Do this and Andrea would be strong enough to stand up to anyone, even Mother. Two days would be plenty of time to clear the air between them—on several topics.

Megan? Megan would be laughing that wonderful laugh of hers as she waved her arm toward the sky and told her to *Fly!*

She had to send Megan something.

What should she send to someone like that? A gift basket with a newborn colt in it?

No, she'd send Major Jazzman Wolfson to fetch her in his pretty Bell 429WLG. They would be her two guests at her swearing in. Maybe she could find a way to slip a gift colt into a pretty envelope for thanks.

Andrea and the Sergeant went through the contract together, then the sergeant printed it out, and the dutiful law student in Andrea began reading it through again. Four pages to the DD Form 4, not a single unneeded word. It didn't take long; she was ready.

She loved to fly. And to do it with the very best pilots would be a joy, instead of the horror of crunching out law for the next five decades.

Sergeant James had made sure the risks were well and clearly defined, and they were somewhat better than riding a motorcycle through San Francisco—which she'd never done but she knew the statistics. Uncle Bob had married an ER doctor. Aunt Bob, as she sometimes called herself, was a very respectable Chinese woman and was accepted by the family more easily than her husband. Yet she'd somehow retained her sense of humor.

Andrea didn't *want* any of that nonsense to be part of her life.

Someday she'd find a woman. A true partner. Brilliant, thoughtful, and kind.

She wanted so much that—

Turning back to the first boxes on the contract, she stared at her name.

Andrea Genji Wu. It looked ridiculous. It *sounded* ridiculous. Even the meaning.

Brave, Valuable as gold, Business.

She'd always wanted a nickname, like Uncle Bob, even if it was his real name.

An...di? Andi Genji Wu? Or simply Andi Wu—*Brave Business*. Like *Brave Kick-ass!*

She crossed out her first two names and wrote *Andi*.

Sergeant James reprinted the page and she signed it with a flourish.

ACKNOWLEDGMENTS

"Megan Connelly," a passionate horsewoman and a devoted mother of three (plus two dogs and a husband), really is a training curriculum developer for the FAA. One of her kids, like Miranda, has been diagnosed with an Autism Spectrum Disorder.

Megan's favorite charity is Special Equestrians (https://www.specialequestrians.net/) offering precisely the kinds of services for children as the ranch she founds in the story. As she prefers to remain anonymous, if you wish to add your support to hers and want her to know, send me a message at www.mlbuchman.com/contact and I'll be glad to pass it along.

TAZ FLIES HER COLORS

Long before **Vicki Cortez** *joined Miranda Chase's air-crash investigation team, she escaped her past. Or so she thought. By joining the US Air Force and being assigned to the Pentagon, she merely traded the lethal streets for the brutal halls of power.*

When **Colonel Elizabeth Karen** *took the young airwoman under her wing, little did she know that simple act would save her own life.*

1

The Pentagon

20 years ago

AIRMAN FIRST CLASS E-3 VICKI CORTEZ CLUNG TO HER shredded clothes.

The US Air Force uniform shirt of thin khaki, that she'd thought of as armor for the entire year since she'd first donned it, was in shreds. Buttons were gone. Her bra strap cut. A trickle of blood ran between her breasts where her commander's knife had nicked her as she'd struggled.

But she hadn't been raped.

For a moment, all she could do was blink in surprise. It had been so close. Her belt was sliced, her pants ripped and slid down to her ankles. Her panties slid off one hip.

She stood four-eleven and had plenty for curves on her small Latina frame that had brought her trouble any number of times before she joined the Air Force.

In her old life in San Diego's Lincoln Park, she'd always been ready. Always had a flick knife in a wrist holster and a snub nose .38 revolver in her boot. Inside the Pentagon, she had neither of those.

Because here she'd been safe...or had been foolish enough to think so.

She slowly became aware of her surroundings through the blanket of fear and rage that this was happening. Her back hurt where she'd been slammed up against the handles of the four-drawer file cabinet almost as tall as she was. Her jaw ached where Captain Wilson had slapped her so hard after she'd kneed his balls that she's almost passed out from the pain.

Now, Captain Wilson lay at her feet on the linoleum floor of his Pentagon office—shuddering. He convulsed like he was being electrocuted.

In his back were two thin wires that—in numb shock herself—Vicki followed to their origin. A one-star general held a bulky black weapon with a bright yellow X26 label on the side. She'd been alone with Wilson just a moment before.

And now she wasn't.

The one-star wasn't staring at her barely covered breasts. Instead he was looking at the weapon in his hand as if pleasantly surprised.

"Well, that *is* interesting. I was given this for evaluation as a less-than-lethal solution. It seems to work."

Vicki looked down at Wilson again. He was no longer shaking. Instead he lay like the losing punk in a street brawl, gasping and trying not to puke.

"I want one of those, sir," she looked back at the general. Martinez on his name badge.

He stepped over until they were separated by only Wilson's body. Without a word, he made a show of resetting the safety, ejecting the spent cartridge, and dropping it on Wilson. Then he clicked in a fresh cartridge and handed the weapon to her. It felt ridiculously light, a quarter of the weight of a loaded handgun. Yet she liked the way its fat handle fit her palm.

Vicki managed to keep her clothes mostly covering her with one hand.

"It's called a Taser." His voice was deep and reassuring. Again, he was studying her face not her body.

Wilson mumbled something that sounded a lot like, "Bitch."

Her ankles were mostly restrained by her fallen pants, but she managed to get enough momentum that the impact of her boot's toe had him curling into a fetal ball and groaning.

General Martinez raised his eyebrows in question.

"I didn't want to waste the cartridge," she raised the Taser.

He offered a wintry smile before nodding to himself. "When you have found suitable attire, Airman, present yourself to my office on 4A8." Then he turned on his heel and stepped out of the room, discreetly closing the door behind him.

4A8.

The Pentagon stood five floors above ground and had two below. It was made up of five nested pentagons, A through E, from the perimeter of the open central courtyard to the outermost ring. Ten corridors crossed these radially outward, dividing the building into territories. 4A8 was the fourth floor of the innermost ring along corridor 8. He was awfully deep into the Air Force officer country for a one-star. That was the land of Major Generals and Lieutenant Generals, not lowly Brigadiers.

It was equally unusual for a one-star to be in a mere captain's basement office after hours, but she was certainly glad he had been. She owed him one and Vicki always paid her debts.

But where was she going to find presentable clothes without prancing half-naked down the halls, revealing that she'd almost lost that battle?

That would be intolerable.

If running with *La eMe*—the Sureños of the Mexican Mafia—on the San Diego streets had taught her anything, it was that the least sign of weakness was always a weapon against you. As a child, a Mexico City drug cartel had proven that when they'd cut off her father's head right outside their ground floor apartment's only window.

If someone thought she could be attacked and get away with it, then she'd become a target for every lowlife, awful, garbage-sucking rat.

Wilson groaned at her feet.

"See these?" Vicki dropped open the tatters of her shirt and waved at her breasts. "Every time you see any woman's breasts from now on, you'll think of this pain."

"Huh?" he groaned out. "Pain?"

Vicki wondered quite how stupid he was.

She scooped up his knife from where it had fallen, cut her ruined trousers in half between her ankles, then kicked him with all her might where his dick still hung out of his pants.

After that, she got to work.

2

"LOOKING FOR GENERAL MARTINEZ, COLONEL. HE ASKED ME to report to him." Vicki saluted the woman who sat at the desk in the outer office. She knew that bravado was the only way through this, as she didn't have a lot of other options.

The lieutenant colonel looked at her through large horn-rimmed glasses that made her dark eyes appear larger than should be possible. Her skin was as light as Vicki's was dark, but her hair was nearly as thick and dark—a flowing brunette rather than her own curling black.

She scanned down Vicki's ill-fitting clothes with a look that Vicki couldn't read: neither disdain nor surprise. Simple assessment?

"Best I have on such short notice, ma'am." Wilson's khakis were ridiculous on her, despite cutting off several inches of pants leg, folding under the cuffs, and stapling them. The captain's knife, that she wore strapped to one thigh, only made her other leg look five times too big. Thankfully, he'd been wearing a standard desert camo top, so that had mostly just required changing out her insignia for his, rolling up the sleeves, and tucking in the long tails.

For lack of anywhere to put it, she still carried the Taser.

"You could fit three of you in there, Airman Wilson." The colonel's voice was soft rather than the disdain that Vicki's diminutive size normally drew.

She glanced down at the name badge that should be above her breast but was closer to her rib cage in this oversized shirt, she'd forgotten about that. "Yes, Colonel. Sorry, Colonel. It's actually Airman First Class Cortez." Her name badge was on her ruined uniform now in a garbage can on an entirely different floor than Captain Wilson's office.

Once again the assessing gaze.

"The general asked me to report to him at the earliest opportunity, ma'am." The colonel's look was not comfortable. As if the woman had the power to throw her away with her uniform. Then what would happen?

Her Mama was long dead, a bystander murdered in a grocery store holdup gone wrong. Her gang was in San Diego and would probably kill Vicki herself on sight for leaving to join someone else, even if it was the US military. It was just her against the world. Fine. She'd deal with it as she always had—head on.

"And what became of *Captain* Wilson?"

Vicki considered denying any knowledge, but the stitching on the back of the name badge that itched against her braless breast would make that a tough argument.

Besides, the colonel had known there was a *Captain* Wilson.

"You might try checking your e-mail, ma'am." Vicki remained at attention.

While the colonel looked to her computer screen, Vicki took her first opportunity to glance around.

Colonel Elizabeth Karen by the name plate on the desk —American last names never seemed to make sense to her Mexican ear. Several photos were displayed atop a filing cabinet. She had this thing for animals. A deer with a fawn who looked too young to be standing. A fox staring at the camera. Another of some bright red bird with a crest perched at a winter feeder—like blood against snow.

"Your work?" The colonel's big eyes were back.

Vicki had assaulted a superior officer, an unforgivable crime in the military, even if he'd done it first. But she'd wanted to make sure he never did it again.

So, Vicki had stripped Captain Wilson of more than just his uniform. Then she'd tied and muzzled him, before writing "rapist" across his forehead and chest in thick black magic marker that she really hoped was permanent. She'd dug a digital camera out of his desk, snapped a photo, and sent it to the entire US Air Force Pentagon e-mail list from his own account. Then, with a final kick that she hoped literally busted his balls, she'd left him for others to find. She'd disposed of the spent Taser cartridge along with her uniform so that nothing would be traced back to the general.

Colonel Karen was watching her closely.

"I did what I thought best, Colonel." Now she could only pray that she wasn't about to be arrested and incarcerated. At least in prison, she'd be the toughest bitch there, another skill she'd brought from the street. But until an hour ago, she'd thought she'd found the perfect bolt hole—the US Air

Force. Now? Not so much. The creeps here were simply better dressed.

Vicki slipped her hand into her pocket. The only piece of her past she'd brought into the Air Force with her—the dark-blue paisley bandana of *La eMe*. It reminded her of who she'd been and what she was escaping when the US Air Force was being hard.

"Sadly, you can't fix stupid," Colonel Karen nodded at her screen but made no other move. "You can go into the office. I'll join you as soon as I've arranged for a more appropriate uniform to be delivered. We have standards to maintain here. Take this, it fits your weapon." Then she held out a belt with a holster of unlikely shape.

Vicki stared at her for a long moment to see if it was a trick.

The colonel waited her out.

Taking it from the colonel carefully, Vicki wrapped it around her waist and holstered the Taser. The belt was far too long for her waist. She slipped Captain Wilson's knife out of her thigh sheath and cut off the long tail. When she handed the excess to the colonel, she merely dropped it in a wastebasket.

"Go ahead," and the colonel picked up the phone.

Vicki stepped toward the door, but listened to the colonel.

She...wasn't calling the SFs—Air Force Security Forces— to come arrest her, at least not yet. She was requesting that the smallest size uniform be delivered here, with a new name badge.

Vicki knocked. She could feel the door's heavy weight. There was no response that she could hear.

She glanced back at the colonel still on the phone but had no idea how to read the woman. She'd given Vicki no clues to read her reaction, as if she was leaving Vicki to make her own choices.

Her own choices?

She'd barely resisted her *first* choice: to cut off Captain Wilson's dick, stuff it down his throat to choke the screams, then ram his own blade into his rapist heart.

Ever since the coyote man had made her eleven-year-old virginity his add-on price for smuggling her and Mama across the Mexican border with new identities, that was how she'd always paid them back.

Other Sureños members learned fast that she hadn't sexed her way into the gang and wasn't one for giving out when she didn't want to. Also, that attacking her or Mama earned them *permanent* retribution. Sureños said gang before family, but her core gang had been of two first and always, then the wider cadre. Until a winged-out gang banger had killed her heart in that grocery. That day she became a cadre of one and didn't care who around her went to hell.

Right to the end the Sureños called her Tiny G, like she was a forever just a kid—the Tiny Gangster at only four-eleven. No one in the gang was dumb enough to mess with her though, after she'd made examples of the two brutes sent to "beat her in" as a gang initiation. They'd eventually learned to respect her enough to authorize the enforcer's pitchfork symbol now tattooed on her shoulder blade. The three gang dots for *Mi Vida Loca*—My Crazy Life—were just at the tip of each tine.

But she'd been inside the Pentagon and forced herself to

not do her worst to Captain Wilson. The streets were about power and danger, the Air Force was about discipline.

Unsure if she'd have heard the general's response to her knock through the heavy door, she opened it and stepped in. She could always pretend that she had.

Except there was no one in the office. Damned colonel had set her up by not saying he wasn't back yet.

3

ELIZABETH HUNG UP THE PHONE AND TURNED FOR THE general's office. From the threshold she watched the young woman inspecting the office, not that there was much to see. Other than a picture of his wife—now seven years gone—and a small diecast model of an AC-130H Spectre gunship he'd flown for twenty years, there was nothing personal. And being in attack aircraft development, everything else was classified and locked up.

Her heart ached for his pain that only she could see. General JJ Martinez kept it locked away deep. It was why she'd stayed twenty-four years in the Air Force instead of the four she'd planned—her husband hadn't been pleased at first but at least he'd understood.

Which might be more than she did. The general had been as driven and taciturn the day before his wife was killed as the day after.

You can't fix stubborn either, Elizabeth thought to herself. Lord knows she'd tried.

His call had been brief. "Sending one to you."

The general certainly knew how to pack the maximum amount of information into the fewest words.

Elizabeth had not expected a woman, and a tiny Latina at that.

But the general was rarely wrong.

The way the woman prowled the office had little to do with Air Force training. Her movements were much more feline. She reminded Elizabeth of a mountain lion she'd been fascinated with in the Sonoran Desert Museum. She'd worked as a docent there for a hot Arizona summer before joining the military. After being picked up as an abandoned cub by wildlife rescue, and nearly dying during two attempted reintroductions to the wild, the cat had become a permanent resident. It moved so effortlessly, so silently about the habitat, that it was almost impossible to look away.

This young airman was like that. Prowling the cage of the general's office, little aware that the trap wasn't for her but rather for the general himself. After his wife was killed by a couple of cokeheads robbing her for their next fix, his life became defined by these four walls.

Elizabeth knew that she herself didn't move like this young airman. Her favorite sport was opening a novel and curling up with a cup of mint tea and a fresh-baked scone. Even better, after her husband had tired out both himself and their border collie during a long walk, he would slip into his own chair and Freddie would nap on her feet during the cold winters. DC was so much milder than the land of her Chicago childhood, but her toes had never made the transition.

She stepped into the office and let the door close behind

her. She knew that Airman Cortez would have pinpointed Elizabeth's position and threat level—which was practically nonexistent. A state of being that she'd long since come to terms with.

She selected her habitual one of the two chairs facing the general's desk. As she waited for Cortez to settle, which she didn't do, Elizabeth watched the restless pacing of the mountain lion.

The general had been looking for someone to solve problems for him.

The fact that Cortez had arrived bearing the Taser, that he must have given her, his recommendation was clear. But the final selection and handling of his staff had always been hers.

Unlike most generals, who surrounded themselves with layers of lower ranks to buffer them from the world, JJ Martinez liked getting his hands dirty.

I didn't fly for twenty years to hide behind my desk.

Every member of his staff had to serve a vital function to be chosen.

4

———

Vicki finally gave up. It became clear that she could delay for a week and Colonel Karen would not be the first to speak.

"Fine. Whatev!" She dropped into the opposite chair like it was one of the car seats they'd scrounged into their old warehouse hangout back in Lincoln Park. "Bring it on, lady."

Still the colonel remained silent.

The *colonel! Shit!*

Vicki pushed herself upright and reminded herself for the thousandth time where she was. She was a clerk inside the US Pentagon. So dispensable that she was little more than a lowly gang foot soldier—definitely how Captain Wilson had seen her—but this place was still a hot assignment for her first posting. It definitely beat the "Country Club" of Tehachapi prison where many of her fellow gang members had landed.

"Sorry, ma'am."

"How old are you, girl?"

"Sixt—" She clamped down on her tongue. The question out of the blue had surprised her. "Nineteen, ma'am. Born 1983 in San Diego, California."

The colonel looked thoughtful. "You became three years older when crossing the Mexican border. A new identity. Yet you still graduated with top grades in a new language."

Vicki swallowed hard. No one—with Mama dead—*no one* knew that about her. "How?"

"I read about that border-crossing trick in a novel. But we'll leave that be, shall we?"

Then she hesitated for so long that Vicki almost spoke again, though she had no idea what to say.

"For now." The colonel announced her power. Colonel Elizabeth Karen could have her thrown into the Country Club in a heartbeat. Lying about her age, her identity, and everything else on a military enrollment form was a felony.

Vicki stayed perfectly still to avoid revealing anything else. She had no leverage at all in this situation and this colonel had the power to destroy her and send her back to the streets or worse.

It was intolerable.

Everyone had a secret and she'd been a specialist at finding them out, but here and now she had nothing.

She had to find the weak link on this woman. And maybe the general too. That picture of the woman on his desk. Old. Maybe in her forties like Colonel Karen. Or like Mama would be next year if she was still alive. There had to be leverage here somewhere.

Maybe her best shot was to slip a knife into the colonel and slide out the front door with no one the wiser. She had disappeared into the wallpaper of San Diego, she could do it again in Washington, DC if she had to. No, that general who'd sent her here knew who she was. Where was he now? With the way her luck was running, he'd walk in just as she was knifing the colonel—probably with a bazooka to combat her Taser.

A test? A trap? Was she about to be—

"We will have to temper your gut reactions."

"What?"

Her gut reaction was...in knots so tight at nearly being raped that they hadn't released even a tiny bit. Yet, impossibly, she was hungry. She was an inch over the minimum height to serve, but keeping over the hundred-pound threshold with her high-burning metabolism was a major challenge. Her blood sugar would be crashing soon.

"Let's take a walk." Colonel Karen didn't make it a command, but she didn't make it a question either.

A walk to some cell?

It wouldn't surprise her at this point. Nothing would.

"HERE?" AIRMAN CORTEZ BLINKED AT THE MANCHU WOK sign like it was a firing squad.

"Don't you like Chinese food? We can go somewhere else. But I like this better than the burgers or chicken fast food," Elizabeth offered. Though even those were a step up from the old-style cafeterias that had only recently been replaced throughout the Pentagon. She'd had far too many off-hour vending machine sandwiches in her day.

"Never had it."

"Never had Chinese food? You need to broaden your horizons, Airman. We'll start you on fast-food Chinese because I don't have time to leave the grounds today. There are several good Greek restaurants within easy walking distance."

"Greek? I'm from Mexic—San Diego. The Mexican side of San Diego."

Unlike the first, Elizabeth ignored the second gaff and focused on being affable. "Like the old joke about Jews know where to find good Chinese food, we Luxembourgers can always find good Greek food."

"Luxembourgers like from Luxembourg? People actually come from there? It's like smaller than my boot heel, right?"

"There are more of us in Illinois and Wisconsin than are in the country itself. What do you like to eat?"

"Um, a burger? Burrito is fine too. Whatever."

"Oh, I am definitely taking your taste buds under my personal command." Elizabeth knew it was her normal instinct: nurture with food. And Airman Vicki Cortez still seemed to swim in the smallest uniform that supply could deliver. Though with the knife and Taser, she did look formidable—the way a Pit Bull Terrier did in comparison to her Border Collie, Freddie, though they weighed much the same.

But that wasn't right either. The small Latina was no more a terrier than a mountain lion.

Perhaps a lynx, small, fierce, and so shy that they were rarely spotted.

Yes, she would have to approach this girl, this *terribly* young girl who'd probably never felt young a day of her life, carefully.

"I eat anything."

"Oh dear, Vicki, that isn't right either. Think about flavor, texture, cuisine... I'll lend you a book."

Vicki eyed her skeptically.

"A novel. *Someone Is Killing the Great Chefs of Europe.* It's a murder mystery about gourmet food."

Still nothing.

"You do read, my dear?"

That earned her a reaction, a very teenage eyeroll. The

manner of it stated that Vicki was not a girl who struggled with a second language despite her lovely Mexican accent. This was an intelligent young woman merely looking for a direction to aim.

Or to be aimed.

General Martinez had been seeking someone to deliver his instructions with absolute clarity and his full authority. Yes, with a little training and polish, this woman would do very nicely—additionally bringing a clear threat of force when needed. The Taser at her trim waist looked decidedly outsized.

Her solution to Captain Wilson had been...innovative. The clear labeling and effective broadcast showed quick thinking and the ability to cure a problem permanently despite the risk of official retribution. It all spoke well of her to the general's purposes.

While Vicki had been changing in the bathroom near the general's office, Elizabeth had seen both General Martinez's eyewitness report sent to security of Wilson's attack, as well as the notification of Wilson's arrest.

At least that problem was now dealt with.

A quick search had revealed that Vicki's record was surprisingly clean. Elizabeth expected that trouble found this girl very easily which meant that she was expert at hiding her actions.

Taming Airman First Class Vicki Cortez would not be so simple, but the potential was undeniably there.

6

"You have a meeting." Colonel Karen rattled off an address in BB4.

"Yes, ma'am." Vicki rose from her desk and saluted. Apparently the sarcasm of it was lost as she got nothing for her trouble except a nod of acknowledgement. Basement, B Ring, Corridor 4. That was Army territory.

Why was the general having her sent there? If he was at all. He'd barely acknowledged her existence since that first day. Even the smallest item was routed to her through Colonel Karen.

"Go."

"Yes, ma'am." She went. In the last four months, Vicki still hadn't figured out how to read her. Though she'd certainly read enough of the colonel's damned books. When Vicki had whipped through the first to prove that she damned well knew how to read, the colonel had made no comment. She simply chatted about the book for a bit as if she was genuinely interested in her thoughts, then brought her a new book—every day since.

At the same time, General Martinez had directed her into a crash course about aircraft design, both its history and its future. So, she'd filled her head with dates and statistics, modifications and crashes, Colonel Boyd's fabulous success with the F-16 development and the disaster that was still the B-1B bomber.

Novels to clear your head, dear, so you'll learn more easily by day, Karen had claimed her nights. And the colonel expected a goddamned book report each morning.

A Ludlum thriller—Bourne rocked—earned the same insistent attention as *The Princess Bride*—which was a totally ridiculous read. Though Vicki had built a brief and secret crush on Inigo Montoya: "You killed my father, prepare to die." Maybe not so brief a crush. Going after the Mexico City cartel that had killed her father, whether or not she herself survived, was very tempting.

But those thoughts were interrupted by Asimov's robot and the Foundation books followed by *The Right Stuff* which gave her dreams of space that no Mexican street kid could ever fulfill.

BB4. Vicki took off through the labyrinthine passages of the Pentagon. Once the coding system was understood, it was possible to walk from any office to any other in the vast building in just seven minutes. Because of the general's prime location on the innermost A ring, she could do all of it in under five without running, four when she was in a hurry. Shaving corners, knowing which corridors to avoid because of their high traffic, and leveraging where the bisecting half corridors sliced across the structure—she had it down.

There was no marker on the basement office door except for its location code.

She knocked and stepped in.

Calling it merely cramped would be a kindness. The table at the center of the six seated men was no bigger than one of those fold-up card tables for four. There was no seventh chair nor space for one.

She was also the only one in the room who wasn't a flag officer.

Vicki saluted and promised herself that she'd keep her mouth shut.

General Martinez was the only one to return the salute and she dropped into parade rest in front of the closed door.

He then turned back to their conversation as if she didn't exist.

Their speech was neither soft nor fast. These were men used to giving orders and never having them questioned. Yet, although they all outranked Martinez, they didn't question her arrival other than by that single look.

Two Marine major generals. One Navy rear admiral. A three-star Air Force lieutenant general. The last was civilian.

No Army here, yet they all were deep in olive-drab country. In the basement. What the hell was going on?

The civilian behaved a little like a drug dealer. Secret meeting, trying to be all casual-cool about what he was selling but doing such a clumsy job of it that any New G street runner would scoff at him—then heist his watch and wallet without him even knowing it had happened.

One of the Marines and the Rear Admiral were definitely ready to take the hit already. Whatever drug the guy was dealing, they wanted a big taste.

Then she began to listen. And the more she listened, the more absurd the conversation became. It was as if everyone in the room was ignoring the data that she'd spent the last four months absorbing.

Then it reached the point where the "dealer" was merely making numbers up.

"Only two hundred billion for full life cycle deployment of three thousand airframes. The next two thousand after that will cost almost nothing. It will cover the needs of all three forces for the next fifty years with seamless crossover."

Vicki couldn't cover her snort of laughter.

All faces looked her way.

General Martinez looked at her deadpan. "You have something to say, Airman?"

"No, sir." She snapped back to parade rest.

He faced her for a long moment, then looked away as if dismissing her. For four months she'd found no way to impress him, and now he was dismissing her. As if disappointed. That *couldn't* be allowed to happen.

"Except, sir, if I may?"

He turned back but offered even fewer indications of his thoughts than Colonel Karen typically did. All he did was nod for her to continue.

"I would ask about the F-117A Nighthawk, sir."

"One of Lockheed's greatest achievements," the three-star Air Force said and the plane-dealing rep nodded happily.

"What's your question, Airman?" Martinez asked in that changeless tone of his. Neither admonishing nor complimenting. So perfectly neutral that he silenced the others who were already trying to forget about her.

"The F-117A was developed using numerous existing components from the F-16 Falcon and F-18 Hornet projects. Those sixty-four aircraft were built with a total program cost of seven-point-two-billion dollars. It was highly specialized to a single task—supersonic stealth attack. It was outdated in twenty-two years and retired in just twenty-five."

She had their attention—but she'd seen friendlier meetings between the Sureños and the Norteños chieftains. Several of them appeared ready to squish her under their bootheels. Yet she couldn't seem to shut up because their facts were just lost in the ozone.

"To argue that the same company, using the same methods, is going to deliver fifty to eighty times as many airframes of a generalized aircraft that will somehow magically meet all three of your forces' needs—Air Force, Navy, and Marines—with significantly more complex, mostly original components for just twenty-eight times the cost, rather than fifty to eighty times, strikes me as a fine plot for a fiction novel, sir."

As others opened their mouths to protest—the rep's looked closer to a snarl—Martinez dismissed her with a "Thank you, Airman. You may go."

And Vicki knew in that moment she'd screwed up.

Billions. *Hundreds* of billions! They tossed around numbers like they were chucking piñata confetti. The stupid jet was going to cost them at least five-hundred-billion dollars if they approved it—and were incredibly lucky. She'd bet her next paycheck that the full life cycle cost was going to crash land closer to a trillion. She'd tried, but there was no way to constructively think about such money; it was roughly the annual gross domestic product of Mexico—all of Mexico—for one stupid plane.

She didn't understand anything.

Habit took her back to the general's office, nothing more.

Colonel Karen cast a worried glance her way, but all Vicki could do was sit at her small desk and glare at the screen. She could check the numbers but she knew what they were and she'd made no mistakes.

But they'd ignored her. Dismissed her.

Because she was a four-foot-eleven Latina. So easy to ignore. Meaningless.

"Why the hell did you send me down there?" Vicki didn't look up.

Colonel Karen spoke softly. "The general told me to send you precisely one hour after the meeting started."

The general.

The one who'd kept her from being raped.

"Well at least it wasn't physical this time."

"What was that?"

Vicki ignored her. She'd certainly been slammed up against the *metaphorical* wall and been treated like some worthless bit of chaff who could be thrown away—

"Those idiots are going to buy it," General Martinez growled as he walked into the outer office.

"Tell me something I don't know." Then Vicki realized who she was talking to, shoved to her feet, and saluted. "Sorry, sir." With Colonel Karen she'd created a more casual relationship through talking about books. But that certainly didn't extend to the austere general.

"At ease. Well, we gave it a good try. I hoped that having a mere Airman First Class point out that they were idiots who were being lied to might have some effect."

Vicki blinked and struggled to understand how the world had just shifted.

She hadn't been used and thrown away.

Martinez had been honing her into a weapon for four months specifically for this moment—to no avail.

Why? Why hadn't it worked?

Because they hadn't cared about what she thought.

"Would it have been any better if Colonel Karen had gone in my place?" But she shook her head before he could answer. "No. She's not a weapon. I'm a weapon."

"You're my," he glanced at her hip and offered the tiniest glimpse of a smile, "Taser."

She slid her hand onto the butt of the handle. She'd worn it every day since he'd given it to her. The general had tromped on security when they'd tried to stop her on her first full day reporting to him.

Vicki had only used it twice since. It had proven wonderfully effective. Word had traveled fast about the dangers of grabbing her ass without permission.

His "Taser." That she could get down with.

"What's next, sir?"

7

"How do I become an officer?"

Elizabeth Karen looked across at Vicki. Her question had come out of the blue, except Airman Cortez never did anything arbitrary—not even ask a question.

The airman had been quiet for a week since the failed meeting, sharing even fewer thoughts than normal. And now? It was a heck of a question.

"You need to attend OTS—Officer Training School," Elizabeth answered. "Though I didn't because I went through college on a ROTC program instead."

Vicki continued to watch her with no change of expression.

"I have degrees in education and working with the hearing impaired. My 'for fun' classes were math and physics—which I suppose is how I came to the general's attention. I handle most of his training sessions. I joined the general's staff when he was still a major and I was a brand-new second lieutenant." And she wasn't sure why she'd said all that. Sometimes the airman made her nervous. "But you need a college degree before OTS."

"College." Vicki's voice was flat, as if it was a foreign word she'd never tried to say before. Apparently it was the only word she'd taken from Elizabeth's entire history.

"Yes, to become an officer, you need a four-year college degree, and then Officer Training School if you didn't go ROTC." Elizabeth wished that she could read Vicki's thoughts but she kept them as well hidden as General Martinez.

Sure enough, Vicki was chewing on that in silence.

Perhaps Elizabeth could simply ask. "Why?"

Vicki stared intently at the linoleum floor between their two desks. "You. The general. The men in that room. You're all officers. You lot hold the street rank, all the power. I'm no more than a New G here."

Elizabeth wasn't sure what a *nugee* was—or, *new gee*? Now she understood, at least the *new* part. Yet she had no power herself. Her power actually came solely from controlling all access to General Martinez.

She flicked a finger against the colonel's bird insignia on her blouse's epaulet loops.

"This isn't power, Vicki. Knowledge is power. So learn."

"Me?" Vicki looked at her in surprise.

Elizabeth turned to her computer, ran a search, and emailed it over.

"Night school? Online classes?"

Elizabeth ran another search, found something better, and sent that too. By the time Elizabeth looked back, Vicki was clicking through options and studying the screen intently.

"Full coverage of education for enlisted personnel through the Community College of the Air Force?" It was as many words as Airman Cortez had ever said at once.

For the next hour, Elizabeth worked in silence, broken only by the occasional fast rattle of Vicki's keyboard. As she was leaving for the day, she glanced at Vicki's screen and recognized the college application from helping each of her children with their own.

"Need a hand?" She knew how unlikely it was that Vicki would ask, or accept the offer.

"Shit, Colonel. No, I got this easy." Vicki didn't look up as she continued filling out the application. Then in little more than a whisper, "You just might be okay."

Four months they'd been working together. As far as Elizabeth knew, it was the first time Airman Vicki Cortez had said anything nice about anyone.

It was odd. For her entire drive home, Elizabeth wondered if "might be okay" could be the highest compliment she'd ever been paid.

8

"What's this?"

"A farm. A small one. My home."

Vicki peered out the window of the colonel's car. She'd never seen anything like it.

She knew cities. Mexico City, San Diego, and DC had taught her how to navigate where she was welcome and where she wasn't. In the barrios she'd blended in, belonged just like any other daughter of a cartel's drug mule. After Papa's execution and fleeing north with Mama to San Diego, she blended in almost as effortlessly, as long as she stayed on her side of town. DC was a total clusterfuck. She wasn't white and she wasn't black so *nobody* wanted her around, not that she cared a rat's ass about any of them.

Her "Cadre of One" was doing just fine.

Her experiences with nature had both been blessedly brief.

She'd walked across the border when she was eleven through the tough, dry hills north of Baja. At fifteen, due to the eighteen-year-old age of her American identity as Vicki Cortez, she'd done BMT—Basic Military Training. Lackland Air Force Base in San Antonio, Texas, was almost as harsh as the Baja hills.

"It's so...green." Tall trees masked Colonel Karen's house from the road. Past them, it looked like she'd expect a farmhouse to look—two stories of white clapboard. "It's big."

"Only my husband and I live here now. Our children have moved on."

"What do you do with all the space?" Her entire gang couldn't have filled the house. And there was a barn almost as big.

Then she looked at Colonel Karen's smile.

"Books," Vicki answered her own question.

The colonel laughed, "Thousands."

"And you've read them all."

The colonel parked under the trees behind the house. "My TBR is substantial. But if I ever retire, I'll have plenty to read."

"TBR? Totally Bitchin' Reads?"

"Close enough. To Be Read sounds so mundane by comparison."

The colonel showed her around the property, a kitchen garden bigger than her family's old apartment in the Mexico City barrio—by maybe ten times. A trio of fifty-foot polytunnels where her husband grew food for local restaurants.

"Will I meet him?"

"Not today. He's out making deliveries. He must have taken Freddie with him. That dog does love a truck ride."

"Good." Vicki didn't know if she was up for more

strangeness. And her experience with dogs were mostly feral, hungry, and lethal in packs. The military war dogs she'd seen training at Lackland only confirmed that they were dangerous.

Inside the house was the wonder. In room after room every section of wall that wasn't window was bookcase.

"Knowledge is power, huh? You must be super powerful."

The colonel laughed again. She did it so easily, as if it was somehow natural to her. Vicki wondered what it might feel like to laugh like that. She'd tried it in the mirror of her apartment and it just came out weird.

She went back to inspecting the books but the titles didn't make any sense, even after she pulled several out and inspected the covers.

The Charm School had a pirate and a woman in a crazy old-fashioned dress about to kiss on the cover. Nothing about how to charm idiot generals.

A whole series of military warfare titles had half-naked men on the covers.

"These aren't about power," the colonel brushed a hand along the spines as if she knew each one personally. "They're about joy, exploring ideas, and having fun."

"Fun." She remembered *fun*. It was what little kids had, playing kickball on the narrow street, until their father was beheaded right there as an example, leaving a blood mark that could never be erased.

"Yes," Colonel Karen stated as if she still believed in such things.

Vicki selected another book at random. *The Prince of Midnight* had an unlikely broad-chested man close behind a woman. He'd pulled her sleeves down off her shoulders, her breasts would be next, and then he'd—she slammed the book back onto the shelf.

"It's a romance."

Vicki walked away and stared out the window.

She knew what "romance" was. It was hot, sweaty, and fast. It happened in dark corners. Quiet so that the rest of the gang wouldn't overhear though everyone would know and smirk afterwards.

Motorcycle gangs who wanted to give oral to earn their wings: black wings for doing a black chick, yellow for an Asian's pussy, blue for going down on a female cop. That was romance.

Or it happened rough and dangerous in the high school locker room when she'd been foolish enough to be caught alone. After finding their top running back on the fifty-yard line choked to death on his own dick, there'd been much less trouble for the school's girls.

Pushing out through the door, she stumbled to a halt on the wide porch.

The silence was like a wall. And the emptiness. The house was surrounded by a big city block of grass mowed as neatly as the National Mall, but with *no* people. In every direction beyond that were broad fields of chest-high grass and rolling hills.

Was this place safe or a terrible isolation danger that she had no training to recognize?

She'd always run. On the streets, she'd learned how to make sure she was always the fastest. During track and field in high school, she'd held every long-distance record for the girls and most of the boys too. The Lackland trainers had tried to run the little Latina into the ground but she'd showed up their asses. Now, every morning before work, she ran 10k: Pentagon to the Capitol Building and back.

Here you could run in a straight line and *never* stop. Barren wasteland like Stephen King's *The Stand*? Or calling to her? Could she run to...what. Freedom?

The screen door creaked behind her and Colonel Karen handed her a glass of iced tea before sitting in one of the wooden chairs. It's something Mama would have done.

"Why did you bring me here?"

9

Elizabeth Karen studied Vicki Cortez's stiff spine as she stood with her toes hanging off the very edge of the porch as if she was a scared rabbit ready to leap away at the first chance.

"I wanted you to see that there was more to the world than the halls of the Pentagon. This," she waved her own iced tea though Vicki wouldn't see the gesture, "is my sanctuary."

"Why?" Vicki turned to face her.

"It has my books, my husband, and our dog. I raised my children here. It's filled with good memories and is my home. I feel safe here."

"Safe." Vicki finally came to sit in the other chair, though perched as if still ready to bolt.

"I've never met someone who could put so much meaning into a single word. Not even General Martinez."

"I've never been somewhere I felt 'safe.' And home? Lost that shit years ago."

Elizabeth knew better than to question Vicki's "never." The girl was so like the general, every word was precise.

"How did the school application go?"

"I'm in. Signed up for classes this morning."

Elizabeth managed not to sigh. She'd thought that Vicki would have mentioned that on the drive out, but the girl rarely spoke without prompting.

"Which classes?"

"Calculus 101. Physics. Some chemistry. There's a lot of metallurgy in planes. I asked if I could just read the books and take the final, but I think that makes their little brains hurt."

"Did you sign up for any humanities?"

"What like psych or English lit?"

"Yes."

For perhaps the first time, Airman First Class Vicki Cortez smiled at her. Really smiled.

Then she waved her iced tea toward the house behind them.

"Why should I, when I have you?"

10

A MONTH LATER VICKI BARELY RECOGNIZED HERSELF AS SHE leaned into her morning run on this blue September morning. The route was the only thing that *was* familiar.

Her morning 10k run was down to Long Bridge Park, then cross over the Potomac alongside the familiar roar of the early traffic. Swinging wide around the Tidal Basin, she'd throw a salute to President Jefferson, then up the length of the National Mall, around the Capitol Building Reflecting Pool, and past Ulysses S. Grant's monument— who she didn't salute because of his role in the Mexican-American War. It hadn't been enough for the US to steal Texas from Mexico; Grant had helped them grab everything all of the way over to California as well.

Everything, absolutely everything else about her was different.

She'd made Senior Airman yesterday, with General Martinez himself requesting the honor—the freaking *honor* —of pinning on her new three-stripe insignia.

The Community College of the Air Force courses weren't like high school, they actually made her work for it, which was new too. It had taken a while for her to find the nerve to ask, but Colonel Karen had been a big help getting her started in physics. It was a beast. That was the one subject she needed most after aerodynamics to keep the general happy. If she kept him happy, it looked as if she'd be...safe. She still wasn't sure about that word.

And, in addition to continuing to feed her books, Colonel Karen had dragged her to enough restaurants that she could now tell an authentic one in a dozen cultures just by smelling the spices wafting out their exhaust fans as she ran by. The dives were usually the best and most real. Though she still didn't get why a Luxembourger from Chicago was so nuts about Greek food.

Three times over the last month General Martinez had sent her to meetings, once without him at all. Resisting the temptation to use her Taser on both majors and the captain in that meeting, for not believing that she knew more about airborne lasers than they did or ever would, was a challenge.

She had finally slammed the weapon down on the table to get their attention, and then kept them there straight through lunch while she'd lectured for three hours to get them up to speed. By the end she estimated that they'd accepted her expertise—and hated her guts. She was down with that.

That evening as she left, the general had smiled at her. Actually smiled.

It was all she needed. She was officially his Taser and now she felt it. She belonged.

Today the kilometers had ripped by. She'd run back over

the Potomac and was almost to the Pentagon's south entrance. Today she would begin—

A high whine filled the air. Looking up she didn't see anything. Then a motion caught her attention. To her left...and *low!*

A jet. A Boeing 757 passenger jet was trying to land on the west parking—

But its engines were definitely *accelerating* not slowing.

No more than a couple hundred meters away, it skimmed over the highway and slammed into the ground floor, disappearing into the building like it wasn't there.

An attack!

Navy and Defense Intelligence Agency were history, some part of her cataloged. Like the bullet to Mama's heart.

Knowing she was too late again, Vicki was halfway to the entry point, already streaming smoke and fire, when the geometry problem that was the Pentagon sunk in.

The plane had hit at the ground floor between corridors four and five. But when she traced the line back to where it had passed over the highway, it hadn't gone in straight. It was angled toward—

Vicki knew about rats and sinking ships, or at least about gangs scattering away from a heavy load of "Jeeps Riding"— SUV-mounted law enforcement. It could be bad, people trapped and caught.

Trapped!

She followed the line of smoke roaring up into the September sky.

Vicki spun and raced away from the wreckage. Choosing an obscure security checkpoint that led into the basement, she pounded down the ramp.

Underground, she sprinted down corridor B2, counting rings as she headed for the building's core K, J, I, H...

At B2D, she didn't slow, instead she caromed off a wall and two visual technicians who looked at her like she was an alien about to eat them alive.

Hitting the next ramps, wide enough for twenty to walk abreast, Vicki drove upward, her feet slapping echoes from the hard walls.

Out of breath. Didn't matter.

Her legs burned from this extended sprint after a long run. Push harder.

The pain in her side. An old friend.

Basement, Mezzanine, 1, 2, 3...

She burst out into 4A8, digging deep into a hard kick until she reached the general's office.

No alarms in this part of the building—yet.

Colonel Karen? Not at her desk.

She shoved open the door to the general's office.

"Where is she?" Vicki was not going to lose her.

The general glanced up at her. "You're out of uniform, Airman."

She slapped for her Taser, except it wasn't there. She was wearing an Air Force t-shirt and gym shorts. Weaponless, she slammed both fists so hard on his desk that his wife's picture jumped and fell over.

"Where is Colonel Elizabeth Karen?"

"She is running an errand for me."

"Answer me or you'll be KOS!"

"KOS?" the general asked in that fucked-up ultra-chill way of his.

"Gang speak. Kill on Sight. It means you're goddamn dead if you don't tell me where she is. Now!"

"What is the urgency?"

"Hello! Did you miss that a passenger airliner just flew into the other side of the building?"

He rose slowly to his feet. "Where?" At least he didn't doubt her word like every other dead-brain here.

"1E4 or 5, but angled this way."

"I sent her to 5E5." Fifth floor, outermost ring, corridor 5. Directly above the crash.

Vicki turned and bolted out the door before the general had time to circle his desk at a run.

11

THE SMOKE GREW HEAVY BY CORRIDOR 6 AND WAS MAKING IT hard to see. Stragglers were coming out of the haze in groups. Everything was screwed up because of a major renovation project, but Vicki found her way through.

A voice was calling somewhere behind her...

A voice calling people to safety. That was for others —not her.

She ignored it, ducked low, and plunged in. Being small let her dodge between people, fallen light fixtures, and scattered slabs of ceiling acoustic tile.

Her throat hurt and she dug her bandana out of her shorts pocket. The paisley blue was the last remnant she had of the Sureños—the southern California Mexican Mafia. She kept it to wipe the sweat away when she ran, and to remind her of the only place she'd ever come close to belonging.

At a water fountain she stopped and dug out her bandana to soak it

Close behind her, someone soaked a white handkerchief in the same water.

She startled to realize that the general had been following her since she'd dashed out of his office.

"What are you doing here?"

"Helping you find Colonel Karen." The general stated it as if it was a simple fact.

No one ever helped her. Except he had. Many times since Captain Wilson's office, even if she hadn't recognized it. She wrapped her bandana around her mouth. Just like the old days, only her eyes showing.

"Not very regulation, Airman," he said as he tied on his own white one.

She brushed a hand over the gang colors. It was strictly forbidden by military code. "Just flying my colors, General."

"Go!" He nodded down the corridor past her shoulder.

She turned and quickly led the way.

12

COLONEL ELIZABETH KAREN WONDERED IF SHE WAS GOING TO die here.

She hadn't seen the impact, she'd been facing the wrong way, but Major Markum had.

Instead, her chair had straddled across one of the building's expansion joints between two separate pours of concrete. One side had dropped vertically by a foot, throwing her into the table. Her left arm wasn't functioning. Dislocated or broken, she was too shaken up to tell.

It was simply...wrong that something as substantial as the Pentagon could move like that.

Markum was kicking at his office door, to little effect—the floor's shift had jammed it hard.

He'd shed his jacket and pressed it against the gap along the floor, but it only slowed the smoke now coming in.

"A plane." She felt like Vicki, stating so much in so few words. A plane hitting the Pentagon was going to be the way she died. Odd. As if she was in a thriller novel.

"I can't believe it. But that's what I saw." Markum spoke between grunts as he raised a heavy metal chair and repeatedly beat it against the door. "It seems crazy. But it hit. Somewhere below us. Terrorist attack? Must be." Each punctation mark was another slam with the chair. But the wood was stout and the door was designed to open inward.

"The wall."

"What?"

She'd said something just now. But she couldn't recall what it was. Two words. Elizabeth was dizzy with smoke or maybe she'd hit her head. Or maybe...

"The wall." That was it.

A pounding sounded to left. From the next office.

Almost the same rhythm as Markum's pounding. The same as her pulse throbbing against her temple.

She went to her knees as she turned to the wall and stared at it.

The pictures on the wall bounced and shuddered.

"The building," Markum cried out. "It's collapsing."

"No." The pictures jumped again.

A boot punched through the drywall sheathing.

Again! This time blasting a larger hole.

A moment later, a face mostly blocked by a dark blue bandana looked through the hole. Then, good Lord, Vicki herself forced herself through the narrow gap and rushed over to her.

She didn't waste time asking how she was. Elizabeth doubted she could have answered.

Vicki pulled her to her feet and dragged her toward the gap in the wall as more kicks widened the hole.

Markum followed close behind her, on the side of her bad arm, he couldn't help as she slithered through.

With her general leading the way and her good arm around Vicki, she staggered through the smoke and wreckage. It was only when she breathed the fresh air outside that she allowed herself to collapse.

13

"ARE YOU SURE?" VICKI WHISPERED ALMOST INAUDIBLY UNDER the choir singing "God Bless America."

Colonel Elizabeth Karen could tell how upset Vicki was simply by the fact that she was repeating herself. For the tenth time, she reassured the girl she was.

They stood in the ranks of thousands before the Pentagon's river entrance. October 11th, one month after the plane crashed into the building, they'd gathered to hear the President's speech at the mass Remembrance Service. It marked the end of a month of mourning. Tomorrow, the repairs would begin.

It had seemed fitting to her that today was also her own last day in the Air Force.

"I have things I want to do, Vicki. I set out twenty-five years ago to help the hearing impaired. To help them live better lives. The attack made me realize that it's time I started doing that before *my* time runs out. I want to volunteer at a zoo again. We have a little family resort in

Wisconsin that I haven't seen in far too long. I miss being around my fellow Luxembourgers."

She looked away from the spectacle and down at Vicki.

"I'm giving my job to you."

"Which job?"

"It's up to you now to protect General Martinez."

"Protect him? The man kicked down a wall to get to you."

Elizabeth smiled. "And who gave him the idea?"

Vicki grinned back. "Well, it was from the structural engineering book you've been helping me with. They gave the example that drywall sheathing had immense lateral strength but low perpendicular shear strength. That meant—"

Elizabeth laughed.

"What?"

"Airman Cortez. I'm going to give you one last command."

"Yes, ma'am."

"You've been flying below the radar your whole life. Just like that foul airplane that flew into this building. Illegally crossing out of Mexico and changing your name. Graduating high school and entering the Air Force when you were really only fifteen. And now you're convinced that you're faking your way through your job. How you haven't destroyed yourself already, I don't know."

"Me either, ma'am," Vicki's rare smile flashed for a moment before disappearing once more.

Elizabeth faced her directly. "You're too good at what you do to make the same kind of ugly waste of life that they did. You're better than...that!" she waved her arm cast toward the destroyed section of the Pentagon. "You saved my life. I'm sure that at some future date you will save the general's. I just know it. All I'm asking is that you be there to do that. If you are, I can retire without worry. We women are the ones who keep him safe."

Vicki was silent through the rest of the song, the breakup of the crowd, and their return to the general's outer office so that she could finish cleaning out her desk.

It wasn't until she got home that night that she received her answer from Vicki.

Tucked deep in the box of her personal belongings from the Pentagon was a brand-new blue gang bandana that exactly matched Vicki's.

There was a simple note tucked inside:

Cadre of two.

It was signed *Amor y Respeto*—gang-slang Spanish meaning "Love and Respect."

No longer in the Air Force, Colonel Elizabeth Karen (retired) knotted the bandana around her neck to fly her own colors, called for Freddie, and headed out to the garden to join her husband.

ACKNOWLEDGMENTS

For "Elizabeth Karen," a 35-year educator of the hearing impaired and people with cognitive disabilities, and a huge reader. Thank you for sharing of yourself to help me create this story.

Elizabeth has been a long-time supporter of, and volunteer for www.bestbuddies.org. As she prefers to remain anonymous, if you wish to add your support to hers and want her to know, send me a message at www.mlbuchman.com/contact and I'll be glad to pass it along.

AFTERWORD

I can never sufficiently thank the five people who shared their stories and their quirks with me. That they were willing to share these with all of my readers is both wonderful and humbling.

Each of these stories would have been so much less without you.

Thanks! M. L. Buchman
North Shore, MA, USA
October 2021

THE PROCESS

Each of these wonderful people agreed to a lengthy interview. I asked a wide variety of questions including:

- Physical descriptions and issues
- Travel history: US and international
- Nicknames
- Professional and *weird* skills
- Hobbies
- Superpower / mental processes
- Favorite sayings
- Favorite recreations
- What they are fanatic about
- Pets, homes, cars
- ...and so much more

They also had to sign a release stating that I could then do almost anything with their character: hero, villain, they might die...

Then I went away and wrote the stories.

Except for the occasional follow-up question, they had no input into their stories. They did *not* read them pre-publication. These are purely works of fiction that happen to be inspired by five wonderful and interesting real-life people.

I did my best to pair each individual with the appropriate Miranda Chase team character. I also strove to honor my perceptions of each person as well as I could.

I can only hope that they enjoy these characters and stories they inspired as much as I did meeting and writing about each of them.

Thank you for your trust.

MIRANDA CHASE SO FAR

AVAILABLE IN EBOOK, PRINT, AND AUDIO

MIRANDA CHASE #10 (EXCERPT)

IF YOU ENJOYED THAT, HERE'S A TASTE OF
WHAT'S COMING IN 2022

MIRANDA CHASE #10 (EXCERPT)

23 Days After the end of White Top
Washington, DC

"Pull to the curb here!"

CIA Director Clarissa Reese's driver obeyed and slid out of the thick Friday night traffic on Columbus Circle. He eased over a block shy of the George Hotel. The US Capitol Building glowed orange in the sunset; the sun still touched the bronze Statue of Freedom atop the dome so that it shone brighter than anything else in Washington, DC, despite the dark finish.

It was just as well; she didn't want to face...anything.

"Pull yourself together, Clarissa." Her self-instruction wasn't helping. She'd been muttering some version of it over and over for the last month with minimal effect.

Her driver studiously ignored her. She'd long since made

it clear that the last thing she needed was to interact with a security agent who'd never be more than a driver.

It was hard. In the last month she'd lost everything.

With her husband's death, her path to the White House had been blocked. Vice Presidents were *supposed* to be well protected. But not Clark. His Marine Two helicopter had gone down in flames, the bastard.

Instead, the goddamn President had elevated his National Security Adviser to Vice President Sarah Feldman.

That had put Clarissa on the street when the new VP had moved into One Observatory Circle. She never should have sold her goddamn condo, but Clark had been such an obvious shoo-in to the White House that she'd been assured of her future residence for years to come.

Their new MERP—Middle East Realignment Plan—had captured the imagination of everyone from the unwashed masses to all but the most jaundiced Washington elite. Even marginal allies were flocking to the call. President Cole had made sure that the bulk of the credit had gone to the VP.

If the woman didn't screw up, she had the next election in the bag a year out.

Of course, when Sarah ran, she *would* need a Vice President.

Except the scandals—thankfully, all classified top secret but littered with her name—had guaranteed her shut-out of any future chance at the Oval Office. It was clear that "certain parties" would release everything if she tried to run.

Bush's route of CIA Director to Vice President was lost to her.

Clarissa looked back at the George Hotel and did her best to discover some shred of composure. It had gotten harder and harder since Clark's death as she discovered more pieces of herself that she'd lost besides her home and her best path to the White House, like the surprising revelation that she missed Clark himself. Immensely.

Even in death he wouldn't leave her alone.

At the White House's request, she'd drawn up a master list of every known terrorist action by any nation from Pakistan to Egypt against the US, and every CIA counterstroke.

It was supposed to be a strictly internal document, but it had predictably leaked. She'd learned from the disastrous 1974 leak of the dreaded "Family Jewels" memos—that had chronicled hundreds of times that the CIA had overstepped their charter.

This time, she'd made sure that all of the questionable activities were chronicled under Clark's tenure as the CIA Director before her. Sometimes having a dead Vice President for a predecessor and a husband came in handy.

It was always better that they blamed a dead man.

Except, instead of the leak wreaking domestic havoc on release, it had become a key document in the President's proposed MERP. It had justified massive realignments and the disavowal of several long-term Middle East allies with their fingers deep in terrorism.

Rather than shaking the nation, it had inspired it.

It had also elevated Clark's posthumous popularity far past anything it deserved. It was impossible to take back the credit, even for her own operations, that she had so publicly given away.

Clarissa sighed. She was late for her monthly dinner

meeting with Hunter and Rose Ramson in The George's penthouse suite.

She didn't need the influence of the Chairman of the Senate Armed Service Committee. Hunter had lost much of his power in his efforts to block the President's Middle East Realignment Plan because it had voided billions of dollars of foreign arms sales for his no-longer-so-friendly defense contractors.

To say that the contractors and Saudi Arabia, among others, were livid about his inability to quash MERP was a significant understatement.

No, she hadn't needed anything from Hunter since his fall. There was even some question of his holding on to his seat for a fifth six-year term at the next election.

Tonight she needed the sharp mind of Washington's top socialite, Rose Ramson, "The First Lady of DC." Clarissa had a new idea, and while it didn't lead to the Oval Office, it would lead to great power.

She had once promised Rose the future Vice Presidency but, as hard as it was to accept, that was gone. The question was, would Rose still support her if that was off the table? Clarissa would leave it up to Rose to name her price.

Sadly, Clarissa suspected that she herself wasn't going to get any more collected together than she was now.

"Let's get this done already."

A gap opened in front of the car, but the driver didn't pull ahead. He wasn't even watching the traffic. Instead, he stared at his side mirror—ducking low to look upward.

He was so intent that Clarissa finally turned to look out the rear window. Instead of a big truck blocking the lane, she spotted a jet. It raced toward them—where no planes were ever supposed to be.

Downtown DC was the most protected no-fly zone in the country.

An idiot, hoping to be in tomorrow's headlines for buzzing DC, had swooped between the Capitol and the Supreme Court Building, and was now carving a hard turn at Columbus Circle.

A sleek C-21A Learjet painted US Air Force blah.

"Damn, they're low," her driver spoke for the first time since Georgetown.

They were. And fast.

In fact, they were so low that—

The plane raced into the narrow slot of E Street Northwest barely wider than its wingspan.

Below the tops of the buildings.

The roar of its jet engines reverberating along the brick-and-glass canyon shook the car, moments before the wind of its passage slammed into them.

A block down, it veered to the right and flew into the side of a building.

It looked just like a Hollywood film.

The plane disappeared through the wall.

For a moment...nothing.

Just a dark hole where the outer windows and red brick no longer reflected the sunset sky.

Then a fireball roiled out in a massive plume.

A second later, most of the glass on that floor blew outward as the plane exploded.

A cloud of debris rained down on the heavy traffic. Her car rattled as if it was caught in a massive hailstorm when debris peppered the body. A brick embedded itself into the hood, making both her and the driver jump.

Screams of injured pedestrians added to the mayhem of car alarms and blasting horns of fender benders as drivers lost control.

Fifteen seconds later—while the last of the debris still pattered down upon them—a pair of "alert" fighter jets raced low over the city. Not a sonic boom, but so loud that Clarissa ducked despite knowing they were far above her and in better control than the first jet had been. Too little, too late.

When she looked up again, she finally recognized the building that had been struck.

It was The George.

The top floor.

The southeast corner suite—

Clarissa barely flinched as a car slammed into her passenger door. Numb with shock, she couldn't move a single muscle.

She was used to looking *out* that window, not locating it from the outside.

The Learjet hadn't been out of control.

It had impacted the hotel *precisely* where, at this very moment, she was supposed to be having her monthly dinner with Senator Hunter Ramson and his wife Rose. They stayed there on the first Friday of every month to enjoy the penthouse's luxury—after a fine dinner and secret meeting with Clarissa.

Either the defense contractors or the Saudis had just gotten even with Senator Ramson for failing them.

Or both.

Were they after her as well?

———

JEREMY HATED MOVING DAYS.

He lay on the carpet in the middle of a sea of boxes and wondered who had invented the idea of moving. If he found out, maybe Taz could do something about never letting it happen again.

She was, of course, being her usual whirlwind. The three-day cross-country drive in a U-Haul truck hadn't fazed her in the slightest. She was one of those unpack-right-away sorts; he was more of an I'd-rather-die-first sort. It was the fifth move of his entire life: college, grad school, the NTSB Academy in Virginia (all three of which he'd lived in the dorm rooms), Miranda's NTSB team in Washington State, and now the "other" Washington—DC.

How had this happened to him?

Four weeks ago, he'd been investigating the horrific crash of the Marine Two helicopter that had killed the Vice President and hundreds of Walmart shoppers. Happily a member of Miranda's team. Never wanting more.

Now he was head of a brand-new team.

What had he been thinking?

He now served two bosses. He was now a member of the National Transportation Safety Board's headquarters lab team. And, with Taz re-enlisting into the Air Force, he had seconded to—

His phone rang. Please let it be the cable guy. He needed to get online, for even an hour, just to clear his head.

"Are you going to answer that?" Taz swept by, making something perfect along the way.

Really, really done with her rootless life to date, she'd picked out the townhouse condo and was busy making it into a home...for them.

Which was too weird for words.

Jeremy had always assumed that he'd find someone someday. But he'd never thought about being a "them" until a four-foot-eleven Latina had slammed into his life. Someday had become very real and very now.

"No," he hoped he was referring to the phone call and not the future. Then answered it to prove that he was completely onboard, even if he could barely move from lying prostrate on the floor. "Jeremy here."

"Good evening, Jeremy."

"Hi, General Macy." He didn't need a call from their new boss at this moment.

"Did you make it to DC yet?"

"We're fully out of the truck and living in a cardboard forest. Maybe it's a mountain range."

"I know that you aren't technically starting until Monday, but are you available for a launch?"

It might be only a temporary reprieve, but it *would* save him from drowning in a cardboard sea. "Where?"

"E Street NW just off Columbus Circle."

Jeremy jolted upright. "In downtown?"

Taz stopped in mid-zip through the living room, which was a relief to his guilt about not helping.

"Yes. We even have the crash on camera from the Air Force alert fighters that were chasing the jet. It impacted the top story of a downtown hotel."

"We're on our way."

"Good man." When General Jack Macy said that in his "command" voice, it was very motivating.

Jeremy pushed to his feet.

"And Jeremy?"

"Yes sir."

"I don't want to bias the investigation, but it looks like it was one of ours."

"Ours? Oh, the Air Force's." He'd only ever been a member of the unaligned NTSB. Now he worked for both the NTSB lab and the US Air Force Accident Investigation Board as a consultant. "Really?"

"Really." General Macy hung up without another word.

"Holy afterburners, Batman."

"What's up, Wonder Boy?"

"We've got a launch. Here in DC." He began pushing around the boxes, desperately scanning each label. How did they have so much stuff?

"What are you looking for?"

"My field pack!"

Taking a single step, Taz tapped a finger on a big box that had bright red tape instead of the standard brown. It was the only one like that. He vaguely remembered that she'd said something about why it was red, but couldn't recall what.

She flipped out her fighting knife, slit the tape, then slid it back out of sight in that smooth move he'd never been able to follow. She folded back the flaps. Inside were their vests and crash-site investigation packs.

He scooped her against him, rested his cheek atop her hair, and held her tight.

Taz snuggled in close. "This had better work, Jeremy, or I'm going to be super pissed."

"The crash investigation? Why wouldn't it?"

"No, you doofus. Us."

"As long as I get to hold you tight, nothing else matters. No way could I do this without you."

Taz sniffled. "Aw shit, Jeremy. You know you shouldn't say stuff like that to me."

"Why?"

"Because if you keep doing it, I might start believing it."

"Good." He smiled as he kissed the top of her head.

She held him just a moment longer, then poked him hard enough in his ticklish spot to hurt. She broke free and grabbed her pack.

He fished out his own.

"Come on, lazybones. There's a crash, get a move on." And his personal whirlwind was out the door before he had even taken a breath.

———

FOR THE TWENTY-THIRD TIME TODAY, MIRANDA TURNED AND discovered that Jeremy wasn't there.

In utter dismay, she inspected the sprawl of the shattered KC-46 Pegasus air tanker spread down the main runway at Elmendorf Air Force Base. It was a Boeing 767 modified into a flying fuel truck—except this one had become a fuel bomb.

"How am I supposed to do this?"

"Come on, Miranda, you're the best there is. You've done more crash investigations than anyone in the entire history of the NTSB." Andi Wu held a fistful of small orange flags on wires for staking out the perimeter of the debris field.

"No, Terence has done more than—"

"Not according to him."

Miranda sat on the airplane tire that had rolled nine hundred and fourteen meters past the next nearest piece of debris. Andi had laughed that cheery laugh of hers when Miranda had insisted that it be properly staked. Usually her laugh made Miranda feel better, but not today. Andi had done the staking, Jeremy's usual task, without complaint but her laugh reminded Miranda of his excitement about every aspect of a new crash.

Only they weren't here. Jeremy and Taz had climbed into their truck, headed east, and were gone.

For two years she could just turn and there he'd be for whatever she needed.

Andi slipped a hand around her waist. "You know it was time for him to fly on his own."

"Knowing that and liking that are proving to be quite disparate thoughts in my head."

"You still have Mike, Holly, and me."

"I do." That cheered her up some.

"And the new guy should be here in an hour or so."

Miranda shuddered. *New.* Such an awful word. In these last months, her autism seemed to be becoming more reactive, squeezing in harder and harder like a cherry tomato that was going to burst and spray out everywhere with no warning. She *hated* cherry tomatoes for that reason —didn't even like removing them from her salad when a restaurant included them against her instructions.

Even finding a good metaphor wasn't cheering her up.

Everything that was supposed to be getting easier seemed to be getting harder.

Although, perhaps Andi was right as usual.

"Last year *you* were new."

"Last year I was a goddamn train wreck," Andi groaned in that way of hers that said she was half joking. Miranda still didn't always get why, but it was a good measure of Andi's generally positive mood.

"But now you're a good thing."

In answer, Andi kissed her on the ear, then whispered so close that it tickled, "Let's go solve a plane wreck."

"Good idea."

They headed back along the runway to where Mike and Holly were already photographing the debris field itself.

Miranda turned to see if Jeremy was following...and sighed.

Twenty-*four* times today.

Coming in 2022

ABOUT THE AUTHOR

USA Today and Amazon #1 Bestseller M. L. "Matt" Buchman started writing on a flight from Japan to ride his bicycle across the Australian Outback. Just part of a solo around-the-world trip that ultimately launched his writing career.

From the very beginning, his powerful female heroines insisted on putting character first, *then* a great adventure. He's since written over 70 action-adventure thrillers and military romantic suspense novels. And just for the fun of it: 100 short stories, and a fast-growing pile of read-by-author audiobooks.

Booklist says: "3X Top 10 of the Year." PW says: "Tom Clancy fans open to a strong female lead will clamor for more." His fans say: "I want more now...of everything." That his characters are even more insistent than his fans is a hoot.

As a 30-year project manager with a geophysics degree who has designed and built houses, flown and jumped out of planes, and solo-sailed a 50' ketch, he is awed by what is possible. More at: www.mlbuchman.com.

Other works by M. L. Buchman: (* - also in audio)

Action-Adventure Thrillers

Dead Chef
One Chef!
Two Chef!

Miranda Chase
Drone*
Thunderbolt*
Condor*
Ghostrider*
Raider*
Chinook*
Havoc*
White Top*

Romantic Suspense

Delta Force
Target Engaged*
Heart Strike*
Wild Justice*
Midnight Trust*

Firehawks
MAIN FLIGHT
Pure Heat
Full Blaze
Hot Point*
Flash of Fire*
Wild Fire
SMOKEJUMPERS
Wildfire at Dawn*
Wildfire at Larch Creek*
Wildfire on the Skagit*

The Night Stalkers
MAIN FLIGHT
The Night Is Mine
I Own the Dawn
Wait Until Dark
Take Over at Midnight

Light Up the Night
Bring On the Dusk
By Break of Day
AND THE NAVY
Christmas at Steel Beach
Christmas at Peleliu Cove
WHITE HOUSE HOLIDAY
Daniel's Christmas*
Frank's Independence Day*
Peter's Christmas*
Zachary's Christmas*
Roy's Independence Day*
Damien's Christmas*
5E
Target of the Heart
Target Lock on Love
Target of Mine
Target of One's Own

Shadow Force: Psi
At the Slightest Sound*
At the Quietest Word*
At the Merest Glance*
At the Clearest Sensation*

White House Protection Force
Off the Leash*
On Your Mark*
In the Weeds*

Contemporary Romance

Eagle Cove
Return to Eagle Cove
Recipe for Eagle Cove
Longing for Eagle Cove
Keepsake for Eagle Cove

Henderson's Ranch
Nathan's Big Sky*
Big Sky, Loyal Heart*
Big Sky Dog Whisperer*

Other works by M. L. Buchman:

Contemporary Romance (cont)

Love Abroad
Heart of the Cotswolds: England
Path of Love: Cinque Terre, Italy

Where Dreams
Where Dreams are Born
Where Dreams Reside
Where Dreams Are of Christmas*
Where Dreams Unfold
Where Dreams Are Written

Science Fiction / Fantasy

Deities Anonymous
Cookbook from Hell: Reheated
Saviors 101

Single Titles
The Nara Reaction
Monk's Maze
the Me and Elsie Chronicles

Non-Fiction

Strategies for Success
Managing Your Inner Artist/Writer
Estate Planning for Authors*
Character Voice
Narrate and Record Your Own
Audiobook*

Short Story Series by M. L. Buchman:

Romantic Suspense

Delta Force
Th Delta Force Shooters
The Delta Force Warriors

Firehawks
The Firehawks Lookouts
The Firehawks Hotshots
The Firebirds

The Night Stalkers
The Night Stalkers 5D Stories
The Night Stalkers 5E Stories
The Night Stalkers CSAR
The Night Stalkers Wedding Stories

US Coast Guard

White House Protection Force

Contemporary Romance

Eagle Cove

Henderson's Ranch*

Where Dreams

Action-Adventure Thrillers

Dead Chef

Miranda Chase Origin Stories

Science Fiction / Fantasy

Deities Anonymous

Other
The Future Night Stalkers
Single Titles

SIGN UP FOR M. L. BUCHMAN'S NEWSLETTER TODAY

and receive:
Release News
Free Short Stories
a Free Book

Get your free book today. Do it now.
free-book.mlbuchman.com

PLAY THE GAME
THE GREAT CHASE

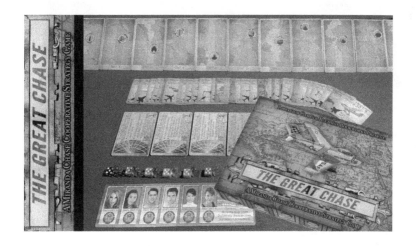

Love the Characters?
Play the Game!
Coming 2022 / Pre-order now!
www.mlbuchman.com/tgc
Tabletop Strategy for Solo-6 players at its best!

CPSIA information can be obtained
at www.ICGtesting.com
Printed in the USA
FSHW012215121121
86201FS